Hospital Eyes
By Corey Duncan Stewart

PROLOGUE

1.

The overhead fluorescent lights flicker on and off in the group room of the Intensive Care Unit in this hospital on the outskirts of San Francisco. I stare out the window into the night with its car and house lights flickering through the haze, while wondering if I'm insane at eighteen.

I think about my friend, Aaron, and how lonely and confused his death makes me feel. I think about the night terrors that I've been having ever since he died, ever since I spiraled down into this depression and tried to take my life. The lights flicker at that thought.

I wake almost nightly, paralyzed and unable to speak, the dark shadowy *presences* standing over me. I feel like they're hounding me, preying on me, like they've been trying to get me to really end it next time.

The lights flicker again, like a *sign*, as though *they're* watching me.

I tried to tell the admitting doctor here about all this, but he just stared at me, raised his big bushy eyebrows over his serious glasses, then said, "Well, we'll get you on some medication that will help with all that."

Yeah, like medication will solve the *demon* thing, or anything for that matter, really. I know what's been happening to me, and I know that I'm not really crazy. Life is what's crazy, not me! And I don't want to be on this brain-rotting medication.

"Aren't you gonna have any of these snacks before bedtime honey?" The heavyset nurse with kind-looking eyes asks me.

"No, I'm okay," I say, staring out the ceiling windows.

"It's all gonna be okay, son," she says, reassuringly as she cleans up the leftovers of our nighttime snack: milk cartons, granola bars and bananas. "You're in the right place, son. God has a plan for you. Don't you worry bout a thing. We'll take good care of you."

My eyes tear up at her simple kindness. But I've heard that said to people before on TV and at church—that God has a plan for them—usually said to people that are pretty tore up and broken, or

God freaks. And if *this* is part of that plan for me, then they can have it as far as I'm concerned, as this seems like a pretty shitty plan. The nurse just smiles, as if she can read my thoughts.

I look back out into the night and think about Aaron and what he'd think of all this. I can see him looking at me with those mischievous eyes, his hair flailing, smiling—he was always smiling, like it's all some eternal joke or something that nobody else got but him. He's now saying something like, *"What in the hell happened, Jackson? Why aren't you in Costa Rica surfing? Why are you in those hospital pajamas looking all pitiful?"* Wish I could explain what happened to me, but he would just shake his head and smile.

"Guys like me and you are screwed buddy," he said to me one night while we were drinking beer and smoking a joint in the hills above Salt Lake City, just after we graduated from high school, trying to figure out what to do with our lives.

"Civilized hell is what we're stuck in buddy. Screw college! Let's go to Costa Rica! I've got a Plan . . ." Then he winked at me, like he just had a revelation.

"Okay," I said, in all seriousness, ready for anything but a 9-5 job, a car payment, and a guaranteed boring-ass existence in the boring-ass town where I grew up. He just smiled at me. He was the mastermind and brains of our operation. I was just along for the ride, the scenery, the laughs, and the drugs and drinks. At that point, I had no direction and couldn't come up with *anything*. Seriously, I'm not a go-getter. Never was. But if you've got an interesting plan, I'm really a great wingman.

So, the plan to make that Plan happen was working a really pathetic job, renting out canoes on the small man-made lake at the park downtown. We'd save money to go to Costa Rica and get jobs as river-rafting guides, live in a hostel on the beach, and learn how to surf. Everyone thought our plan was crazy. But it sounded like the calling from a prophet to me, given my lack of options.

Then one night it all ended. One last acid trip and one drug high too many.

I wish Aaron was here hanging out with me now. He'd at least make me smile or laugh or *something*, and that would be great as this "trip" has gotten too serious, out of hand, and downright shitty. He'd think my situation was funny somehow, look at it as though we were on an adventure, maybe pretend we were undercover reporters investigating the state of the mental health industry and its actual effects on people's sanity. He could make any sorry ass situation entertaining. And if you really think about it, that's like the best skill anyone in the world could have, as *most* of life is pretty shitty and rather boring. I mean, if Aaron were a pretty girl he would've become like a guru to Oprah and stars or something stellar. And I was lucky enough that he was a little overweight and crazy-looking.

The aging intake doctor who checked me in thinks that it's not healthy that Aaron is my only friend and that I talk to him in my head. I could tell he disapproved by the way he sighed and subtly shook his head, then wrote down some notes on a yellow legal pad. Old guys are the most stodgy people ever. Most of them are just grumpy about everything, and they never smile at anything and shake their heads and they sigh a lot, at least around me. But I don't care, crazy or not. Aaron is more interesting *dead* than most people are to me alive. Jesus. Now I'm *sad* and *depressed*. It's a horrible combination that doesn't attract the opposite sex. Oh yeah, I forgot to mention my girlfriend broke up with me too. I think actually I broke up with her, but only because I knew she was gonna dump me soon—I'm pretty good at reading people. Girls want guys who are dynamic and enthusiastic and have the tiger by the tail. Yet most people who play with tigers end up getting mauled, so screw them anyway.

One of the other patients, Koran, I think her name is, is shuffling around the room as though she has lightning bugs in her hospital-issued slipper socks. She's got cornrows, searching eyes, and a pretty if worn-down face that looks like it's seen too much hurt, sorrow and sadness. She moves smoothly through the room tidying up, throwing away napkins and pushing in chairs, while talking to herself under her breath as she goes along.

I watch her out of the corner of my eyes as the lights flicker overhead again.

"Damn *demons* . . ." Koran says to herself, then yells out toward the nurse's station. "Somebody should pay the light bill around here or call an electrician! *How* we supposed to get sane if the lights are always actin' crazy?"

I smile to myself, as she explains to me, "The *devils* come through them lights. Don't you pay em no attention now . . . You hear?"

I nod my head. I believe her.

The intercom weakly crackles on, "Lights out in fifteen minutes."

Koran laughs loudly and shakes her head. "I don't know why they couldn't have just told us that instead of usin' that damn janky ass intercom," Koran says, then shuffles out of the room. "I'm goin I'm goin," she yells from the hallway.

Thinking about her and where I'm at, I feel the tears welling up in my eyes again, and I go back to my room to lie down to figure things out.

2.

My room in the ICU looks like someone has been on a drug binge at the gloomiest college in the country. The walls are shell-shock blue. The dressers and nightstands are made of stained particle board that's warping badly. The bathroom mirror is unbreakable, so we don't shatter it and slit our wrists. The ceiling is water stained. My roommate, a huge man with horribly pocked skin, tosses and talks in his sleep. Tonight, he says, "I don't have a gun?"

I reply, "Thank God." Then, he turns over and snores.

I stand next to the small window in the room watching the cars moving slowly through the streets below like they're in some monotonous real-life video games. Not real objects. Just wandering aimlessly for points that don't add up to anything worthwhile, except maybe the bragging rights of a digital "top score" in your bank account. And who cares about the score anyway when you're dead? I got the high score once playing *Ms. Pacman* at Disney World in Orlando when I was a kid. The goal was to eat "power pellets" to chase away ghosts. I could use some now.

The woman who found Aaron's body at the scene of the accident told the paramedics something strange, ". . . a yellow ray of light was shooting fifteen feet high out of his body into the desert night." His *soul* was that big. Way too big for this world. He was in an awful car crash, and there wasn't a scratch on his body. The cross that he wore around his neck was lying flat on his forehead, as if God had carefully placed it there. Two of our friends were in the car that night. Their bodies were mangled beyond recognition. But not Aaron's. He just lay there dead, peacefully glowing into the night, ascending from the side of the road, his cross resting on his forehead. How do you explain that?

I asked our Mormon bishop about it. He said, "God works in mysterious ways." That's always what religious people say when something doesn't make sense to them and they can't quote the bible. The bishop looked around the church at all the bright windows, and mahogany pews, and then toward the front with its massive organ. It was like he had something better to do, maybe cleaning its bronze pipes. That bleating organ always drove me crazy. I'll bet it drives God crazy too. Even Jesus seemed to be glaring down from his massive cross at this monstrous organ. It was one of the main reasons I stopped going to church. It really drove me nuts the way it droned on, and combined with the congregation singing along; it sounded to me like a bunch of people drowning in the ocean. Besides that, the church service was just monotonous as hell. Church is what made me think that religions just make up their version of God for tired, old people to give them something to look forward to every week. Why would *any* real deity want a singalong like that?

I could tell the bishop thought I was lying anyway, as Aaron wasn't a Mormon and non-Mormon's don't go to heaven or have bright glowing souls that shoot up into the sky when they die. I'd rather hang out with people like Aaron rather than listen to him anymore.

The night Aaron died was the night all this sadness and craziness began for me. I didn't take Aaron's death very well. And I've been desperately sad for a while now. I didn't even go to his funeral. That's how shattered I was. The intake doctor here said that it was "a traumatic event." And if you factor in the weed that I was smoking and the beer—just to calm that sick feeling in my gut—I guess I was the poster boy for a mental break. *Snap!* And just like that I'm a full-fledged mental case, locked up like a medicated zombie.

Of course, I ended up here because of my half-assed attempt to kill myself in a motel room, or until Aaron stepped in. I mean, I was blitzkrieg drunk. In my warped state, I figured it would somehow be easier for my family to deal with it if I killed myself in San Francisco, the home of the Golden Gate Bridge leapers. Doesn't really count if you kill yourself out of state or something, does it?

I lie down on the stiff mattress and stare out into the dark night at the planes circling in the sky waiting to land; like me, I guess. Then I think about when I was baptized at eight years old.

During the laying on of the hands, it felt like a ray of bright light was shooting out of my head through the roof of the church straight up to heaven, just like the woman said about Aaron's spirit ascending. Maybe we had some kind of spiritual connection as well. Growing up I always wanted something magical to happen to me. I always thought it would, but this isn't what I had in mind.

I roll over and think about something I read once, that we're all spiritual beings having a physical experience, not physical beings having material experiences, or something like that. I don't really care about all the material crap. But then I'm pretty spiritually sick right now and don't know what will make it better. Maybe I should pray to the real God? All our society seems to care about is material things. No one gives a damn about real spirituality. I doubt if any of the money-grubbers' spirits will ascend like Aaron's.

All I know is that I don't think I *need* medication. I think I just need some *meaning* and maybe a new good friend who's not a materialistic robot. Somebody with a real spirit who's not been programmed to earn money and achieve success and be a self-centered pompous, egotistical asshole. I mean, like someone who wouldn't even try to help injured animals, or care about the patients in this ward. Or, like Ronald Reagan, would just dump them on the street. I'm going to tell the doctors that.

"No, you can't go telling the doctors stuff like that," Aaron says. *"They'll keep you locked up longer if you go telling them crazy, nonsensical stuff! You've got to tell them that you're going to take your medication, get a job at the bank your mom works at, get a sensible car, start a 401K, and pay your bills. That is, be a productive citizen of society! That's what'll get you out of this hellhole, buddy! That's what they want to hear, not you, talking about demons and spiritual experiences and the injustice of the world! Jesus man, pull yourself together."*

I think about this for a minute before answering him. He's got a good point, really. Nobody wants to talk about spiritual and crazy stuff. If you do, they just tell you about a book you should read or a documentary to watch, just to get you to stop talking. Not even doctors and therapists and parents want to hear about it. They just want you to get a job and stop talking. Like getting a job is the only point to living.

Aaron keeps going on, *"The only way you're gonna be able to tell people about all the real insanity is to write about it. That's the only place you can tell people stuff like this and not be locked*

away for it. If you can write a book, maybe that will give you the

meaning you've been looking for?"

Okay buddy, that's a good idea. Let's write a book about all

this crap.

"That's the attitude I like to hear! First, we need to get you

some notepads and a pen."

You think they'll let me have a pen in here?

"Yes, as long as you tell them things they want to hear, like

you don't want to kill yourself anymore or stab anyone, and you

should be fine. Ask your doctor about it tomorrow."

Okay. This is a good plan.

I look up at the few stars I can see out the window and think

of one of the last nights Aaron and I hung out together. We were in

Arches National Park camping just after graduation and a week

before his car crash. We had dropped acid, and it was mind-

blowingly magical, really spiritual down there in the desert. Once the

acid *really* kicked in, I went off on some mad ranting diatribe about

how I've been lied to all my life about being special, about how *life*

was special, and that made Aaron laugh so hard that he was crying.

"See, I got ribbons at school for doing my schoolwork," I was yelling at the stars, pulling at my hair, drinking beer and smoking a cigarette! "I got stickers at home for doing my homework! I got trophies for playing sports and was told at church that I was a special beam of light! And all I did was what I was told! So, what's so special about that?" Aaron was crying from laughter.

"I don't know, buddy? You tell me," he said.

"Follow me here . . . All they're giving us ribbons for is just doing what we're told!" Aaron howls at this line. "They were just tricking us into thinking we were *special* when really, they were just grooming us to be good complacent workers who don't question authority! Go to school, get crushed with debt, work a boring-ass job, get married, have a couple of kids, chase money until it makes you crazy, get divorced, pay alimony, and then working yourself to the bone until you can hardly move anymore and retire and die . . . What's so *damned special* about that?"

"That's great, buddy. I think you're on to something," Aaron coughed out, wiping away the tears. A storm appeared way off on the horizon with thunder rumbling and lightning crackling across the skyline as though it were responding to my rant. So, I just kept rambling on about how everyone is full of crap, and how material things and the race for money and fame were all phony and empty, and that *love* was the only important and real thing. Aaron kept laughing, and we kept drinking, and as the storm closed in on us, Aaron yelled, "That's right! You tell em, buddy! You *tell* the whole world what a con all this is!" Then he stood up and hugged me, crumpled up a beer can, and threw it into the night. We sat there the rest of the night watching that lightning storm roll in and over us like it was the most beautiful show we'd ever seen, until eventually the heavens opened up on us. That was the first time I felt like there *had* to be a God outside of religion; it was that beautiful.

The fluorescent lights out in the hallway begin flickering again, pulling me out of any transcendent thoughts, trying to banish Aaron out of my head at such moments. *They* see him pulling out this side of me sometimes, and that's a threat to them. *They* just want me to focus on how crappy I feel and how bad things are. And *they* wait for me in the space between dreaming and waking, whispering to each other about my doomed fate.

After Aaron and my friends died, I was flailing. So, my dad got me a job working at a warehouse his friend owned. It had something to do with oil products. It was located in the industrial part of town, and inside it was hot and dirty and grimy. The bathroom had centerfolds from *Penthouse* magazines stapled to the walls. All the other guys there were either drunks or meth heads or dickheads or all three. It really sucked. But then I was a mess and a miserable employee. The warehouse was immense. You could get lost in there, and I did that on purpose almost every day. When I was supposed to be stocking shelves or looking for something, I'd climb up into the rafters find a hiding spot and take a nap. And then when I heard someone calling my name, I'd climb down and pretend like I was working really hard trying to find something.

After a while my supervisor figured out that I was only good at cleaning up spills, and so that's what I did all day. I have a hard time passing up a mess without trying to clean it up, even if I didn't make it. Actually, I didn't mind that task. Someone would spill some oil in the warehouse, and I'd clean it up. Someone would leak some oil out by the gas pumps, and I'd clean it up. Lots of people would spill oil out in the parking lot, and I'd clean that up too. I found all the sweeping and cleaning calming. Later, I would discover that was just a symptom of my obsessive compulsive disorder.

When I was off work, I'd hole up in my basement bedroom at my parents' house, watch MTV, and drink myself to sleep most nights. I even stopped seeing the girl, Caitlin, that I was hanging out with. I was in love with her I guess, or I realize that now, but at the time it was too hard to talk to anyone. People would keep asking me how I was doing all the time, and it all just hurt too much to really tell them; I never seemed to have the right words anyhow. And when I would finally tell someone how I was *really* doing, like my parents, they'd get all emotional, then just sit there silently, or worse, get up and leave the room - we don't really talk about uncomfortable things in our family. I didn't know how to tell Caitlin what I was feeling, or how I felt about her; I guess I was too scared for her to know, to be that vulnerable. I don't care what anyone says; it's really hard to tell someone how you really *feel* about them, especially if you don't know how they really *feel* about you. So, I didn't say anything, and then eventually I just shut her out.

Caitlin had pale skin, strawberry-blonde hair, piercing green eyes, and lips that smelled like watermelon. One night at a party I *tried* to tell her about what I was feeling, but it went all haywire. I was too drunk. The words wouldn't come out in the right order. She just stared off into space, and then tears came to her eyes. I wanted to tell her that I loved her and that everything was okay, that I was okay, but I wasn't. It wasn't okay at all. I stood up and left the party and walked home alone with tears streaming down my face. After that I just kept it *all* in. That was the end of us. I never answered her calls, and so she broke it off, but I can't really blame her.

My parents wanted me to talk to a therapist, but I didn't want to talk to anyone except God, but only to tell him what an asshole he or, to be politically correct, *she* was. They even had a psychologist friend over for dinner one night, and the conversation got around to grief and how devastating it could be. I looked at the three of them and saw that none of them had experienced it to this extent. I stood up and left the table. I'm sure they were relieved.

That's probably when they came up with the idea to ship me off to Oakland to help me get my life back on track at my grandparents' house. I guess they figured it was better for me than sitting in my room staring off into infinity and laughing at things my dead friend said. Maybe they thought the fresh ocean air of

California would wash away the bad thoughts, or that Aaron wouldn't follow me there. It wasn't exactly Costa Rica. Who knows? You can't really know what's going on with others.

I mean, who the hell knows what's going on in other people's heads? For instance, ever since this happened to me, older people have been coming up, putting their hands on my shoulders, and saying things like, "The world is your oyster, son." Or, "You just don't know it, but you've got the tiger by the tail, son." And I guess that when eating a bologna sandwich, while watching a baseball game on TV and drinking a non-alcoholic beer amounts to the excitement in your life, I probably did have the tiger by the tail in their eyes. I wish I could see it that way, but I get confused easily these days.

And so, their bright plan, "Oakland or Bust," was put into motion, and that's when it all started to unravel for me.

PART I

4.

A cover of clouds shrouded the Wasatch Mountains on a dull fall afternoon as I threw my backpack into the car. My dad appeared in the doorway to watch me leave, a look of concern covering his half-hearted wish of good luck. I think he was glad to see me go. One more problem out of sight.

I pulled into the crowded parking lot of the bank at the base of the tallest building in town where my mom works. I had barely left the house during daylight when I was off work since my friends died; the frenzied self-important movement of people made me feel uncomfortable. I entered through the double set of glass doors, saw my mom near the towering gray windows along the far wall of the spacious lobby with its gleaming marble floors. She was wearing her pink outfit, more motherly than businesslike. I flashed my best smile. I could tell that she was worried by her stiff body language, and I tried to put her at ease, acting calm like I was in control.

"I like to see you smile," she said as I approached. "It's been a while. Are you excited about this move? Your grandparents will be happy to see you." She was holding an envelope with money for my escape. But I wasn't sure about anything right now.

"I'm sure, Mom. Can't wait to see them," I said, smiling and wanting to believe it myself. I could see her getting a little choked up as tears started to pool up in her eyes, and she put her hand gently on my arm. I don't think there's anything worse than seeing your mom getting all choked up about you, especially when you're lying to her about your state of mind and she doesn't even know it. I told her that I thought it was for the best, that I was ready for a new start, to put the past behind me and all that crap—all the things I know she wanted to hear and that I wish were true, but it made me feel sick to my stomach.

"Your grandparents are expecting you," she said, kissing my cheek and squeezing my arm. "Be safe and call us when you get a chance." She handed me the envelope, sadness and concern shrouding her, and it just made me feel so awful to see my mom like that. I almost cried.

I thought back to my final year of middle school, the last time I remember my parents being really proud of me. Graduation day stood out.

Everyone was packed into the school's big auditorium. There was a lot of commotion. All the kids were wearing their best outfits, talking loudly with nervous energy. Besides handing out diplomas, the teachers gave citations like, "Most Likely to Succeed," or "Most Popular." Everybody finally settled in, and the commencement began. By the time they came to my name, I was all nervous with sweaty palms. When I got up on stage, my English teacher stepped up to the podium, winked at me and then announced, "Jackson Smith, voted most likely to become an author. Congratulations!" My essay on Robert Lewis Stevenson's *Treasure Island* won first place in their literary contest.

Mr. Christensen stepped over with my diploma and citation and shook my hand. "Good luck, son." For a moment I was light-headed, my ears were ringing, and time seemed to slow down. When I returned to my seat and sat down next to my parents, they were beaming like I'd just won an Olympic gold medal, a Nobel Peace prize, or an Oscar. "We're so proud of you Jackson," my mom said putting her hand on my shoulder. "Yes, good work son," my dad said, nothing less was expected of me. High standards.

The next year I went to high school; I grew a bunch, got acne and felt like a stranger in my own body. Our high school had just absorbed the struggling students from the worst high school in town, closed down that summer. I felt lost and out of place, a little scared honestly, and that's when I met Aaron.

I took the envelope and walked slowly out the door under the threatening sky, slipped into my car. I sat there and tried to convince myself that I could put my life back together, that I could go out to my grandparents and enroll in community college, just like my parents wanted. I'd make new friends, get a new girlfriend, and everything would be okay again.

But once I started driving along the blank stretch of I-80 under the cover of clouds, I couldn't tell if I was running from or chasing the darkness. When I got near Wendover, Nevada, I pulled the car to the side of the highway near mile-marker 100 where Aaron's crash had happened. I got out and walked around hoping to feel *something,* but I just felt empty. I had thought about making a wooden cross to place at the site, like you see at other crash sites, but I couldn't bring myself to do it.

I drove through the night moving across the empty prairie landscape, ending up in a nondescript motel off the side of the highway outside Reno after the seven-hour drive. I was disoriented, couldn't get my bearings, and realized that I was in real trouble since

I couldn't outrun the demons in my mind. What was the phrase, "We only meet ourselves wherever we go."

And as I drifted to sleep, I could feel the *dark presence* standing over me. Through the slit in my eyelids, I could see the television screen full of static in the background. The clock read 3 am. I was paralyzed and terrified. I couldn't breathe and then I *screamed.*

I woke in the morning with a start as a big eighteen-wheeler rumbled by on the freeway outside my motel room. I rubbed my head several times as if I were trying to wake up from a bad dream. I didn't have one, it just felt like I was living one. I sat up and looked out the dirty window of the room toward the Denny's across the street and started to laugh hysterically. It reminded me of the time Aaron and I were at a Denny's in Salt Lake City when all hell broke loose. I swear the craziest things would happen when we were together. It was like we'd create a portal that would attract weirdness into the universe. Tears came to my eyes thinking about it, even though it was a funny story.

It was about 2 am in the morning at the 24-hour Denny's. We'd been drinking beer, smoking weed, and playing foosball all night long in the basement of his house. That was the kind of stuff we liked to do on the weekends, as well as watch this crazy show called *Lions vs. Hyenas*. Aaron loved that show. He had it recorded on a VHS tape, and we must have watched it at least a hundred thousand times or more. He loved the Hyenas and was always rooting for them to win even though he knew they hardly ever did. But when they did win, he'd become all excited and start doing the play-by-play commentary like it was a college football game or something: "And here comes another hyena flying in out of the bushes on the left side, out of nowhere, to help take the lion down! Oh, what a move! The lion *did not* see that coming!" He *loved* that show, and I'd laugh so hard at his play by play that my eyes would water up and my stomach would hurt.

Life sucks when you realize that you can be having such a good time, laughing so hard that you're crying, with no idea that one day coming *soon* you'd be sitting in a dirty, crappy old motel room in Reno all alone crying just thinking about it. They don't prepare you for anything like that in school. That shit happens. After we watched *Lions vs. Hyenas* and finished playing foosball, we had the munchies and walked over to Denny's around the corner to get some pancakes. We were sitting there at the counter a little stoned, when we heard a Harley Davidson come to a screeching halt outside the front door. We turned to look, and suddenly it was like the energy shifted and we were in *The Twilight Zone*. There was a real cute girl with blue eyes and a blond ponytail behind the counter. She was taking our order when her face went pale as a ghost. Then this shirtless, tattooed guy with long hair and wild eyes came blasting into the Denny's, yelling, "Where the hell are my guns?"

I looked over and saw that Aaron's eyes were bulging out like he just realized his ass was on fire or something awful like that. He turned to me with this shit-eating grin on his face and started kicking me in the shin, like, "It's happening. Jesus, it's happening again." And this tattooed guy comes right over next to us and starts yelling at the poor, cute girl behind the counter, just laying into her. "Carrie! You tell me now*!* Where the *hell* are my guns? What the hell? I get out of prison and come home, and all my guns are *gone!* I swear to god I'm gonna kill whoever stole my guns!" You could hear a pin drop in the place it was all so crazy, and poor Carrie just burst out into tears. Aaron kicked my shin over and over again and whispered under his breath out of the side of his mouth, "Do something, dammit! Do *something!*" Holy shit, just the thought of it nearly killed me. Do something. Like I was gonna do something when this guy could have killed me with his bare hands. He wouldn't even have needed one of his guns.

Nobody in the place moved a muscle when all of a sudden, this nerdy-looking manager with glasses came out of nowhere and said to the tattooed maniac, "Okay mister, you need to go!" Like that was going to solve it all. The tattooed guy glared at the manager and yelled, "Piss off, four eyes! ***This is about guns!***" And I swear to god Aaron's eyes almost popped out of his head like it was the coolest thing he'd ever seen and heard in his whole life. And after that, anytime Aaron wanted to make a serious point and get my attention, he'd say, "Jackson. *This is about guns!*" That was the kind of stuff that would happen when Aaron and I were together. It was like we were in a movie that nobody told us they were shooting. Something like that Jim Carrey movie *The Truman Show*.

Another big truck rumbled by on the highway under the clouds that were building up. I pulled my stuff together, checked out of the motel, and started driving again, feeling like I was in a daze on autopilot.

5

I drove west on Route 80 through the Tahoe National Forest. I liked the climb up to 7,000 feet at the Donner Pass. The air was clear and cooler. I stopped at a scenic pullout, stepped out, and sat on the edge of the mountain just breathing in the air. I love the mountains and liked hiking in the Wasatch Mountains east of Salt Lake City. For a moment it felt like my mood had shifted, but once I was back on the road and realized that if I kept driving, I'd get to Oakland today, it turned bleak again. Too much too soon.

The last mountain town was Blue Canyon. I checked into a truck-stop motel there and slept off the rest of the afternoon. As the sun began its descent, I went out to buy a six pack of beer. Like an omen or something, the old grayed-out guy behind the counter of the mortuary-lit convenience store took my fake ID, looked at it for a little too long, glanced over at me, and then said, "Looks like you're *expired*. You should get that fixed son," he added gravely and handed it back to me. He then rang up the register. I looked down at the ID. It had indeed expired. The guy who gave it to me was the coolest guy in high school. He had a kickass car with custom rims, tinted windows, and a stereo system that you could hear from class when he'd pull up in front of the school to pick up his cheerleader girlfriend. His hair seemed like it was always shining, like he literally had a glow about him. About six months ago, I heard that he shot himself in the head with a shotgun. His father had just died in an avalanche while they were skiing together in the backcountry. I mean, if things could turn that bad that quickly for the coolest guy I'd ever known, what hope was there for me.

Back in the dirty motel room, I started to drink to numb the pain. I thought of buying a shotgun, but I couldn't imagine doing *it*. And besides, I didn't know where to get one, especially at night. So, I just sat in silence, staring out the window towards the highway, at the setting sun and the passing cars. I set a picture of me and my friends at our high school graduation up against an empty beer can on the table in front of me. I can't stand being alone, but I don't feel comfortable anymore being out and around people in daylight. They just stare at me, as if they can read my thoughts and see how messed up I am. So, I just kept on drinking with the picture of my friends keeping me company and waiting for the sun to set.

Once the sun went down, I asked the desk clerk about local bars. The closest was a few miles down the road, so I drove there. Country music played from a jukebox in the corner of the dark and smoky room where a couple of guys with homeless tans and hard lined faces played pool and smoked. A few people sat quietly on rickety barstools nursing drinks and watching the football game on the television. I sat down next to them; my reflection from the large mirror behind the liquor bottles, with those sad blank eyes staring back at me, caught me off guard.

"What'll you have darlin?" The kind of trashy, sweet bartender asked, looking at me like she understood my sad eyes. I'll bet she sees a lot of sad eyes in a place like this. She smiled like everything would be all right. "You look too young and too nice to be at a bar like this on a weeknight," she said. That was nice of her. I like older ladies who seem like they can understand your pain. Young girls just look right past you. "Can I see your ID?" I handed it to her, and she looked me up and down. "All right, so what can I get you, *Jason?*" The way she said *Jason* showed that she knew this was a big favor.

"A beer and a shot of whiskey please," I said and suddenly felt more alone even around these down-and-outers like I was trying to be normal when I really wasn't. I felt like I had to go, like I didn't know where I belonged, because where do you go if you can't go home and can't even go to a shitty bar?

"This'll help," she said and smiled as she set the drinks down. "The beer is on me, hon." As I sipped the beer, I realized that this was the most human interaction I've had in a long time, besides my parents. If she were younger, I'd ask her to marry me. I looked up at the football game and thought about going to college like my parents wanted, standing in the student section of a football stadium wearing the school colors and cheering like a madman. I can't see it. And I could recall Aaron saying once, *"What the hell are you gonna go to school for? That's a stupid idea. All universities teach you, is how to take orders from other people and become a complacent and docile employee. You're just going to become an indentured servant burdened by debt with a dead-end job and a dead soul. There's way too much adventure out there in the world than to fall into that bullshit trap! What do you **really** want to do?"*

Surf.

Becoming a surfer seemed like a real thing when Aaron was alive, not a pipe dream.

I thought back to the first time I saw Aaron. It was after school, a couple of weeks into my freshman year. I was heading out the back of the building, so that I could avoid all the clicks of kids hanging out on the front steps, gossiping and talking shit. The football team and cheerleaders were practicing on the field there. I didn't have anything to go home to, so I decided to sit and watch practice for a bit. The air was crisp. The leaves were starting to turn their autumn colors. I could smell smoke from a chimney off in the distance.

There was a group of guys sitting at the top of the bleachers who looked like stoners, with their long hair, heavy metal T-shirts, and ripped jeans. They were all sitting around a guy with wild medusa-like hair, who looked like he was holding court. He had a shirt on that read: "Trust No One," with a flying saucer above it. His hands were moving animatedly, and the guys were listening intently to whatever he was saying. I sat on the bleachers close enough to catch bits and pieces of it.

Suddenly, one of the guys yelled out, "You're full of crap!" With that declaration, all of them started getting up and grabbing their things, shaking their heads as they headed off.

A whistle blew on the field and the football players began huddling. The cheerleaders were practicing a yell, "BE AGGRESSIVE, BE, BE AGGRESSIVE." I didn't feel very aggressive.

"Don't believe me at your own peril!" yelled the guy with the flying saucer T-shirt, as the other walked down the bleachers past me.

"Man, Aaron, you're crazy!" one of the guys yelled looking back at him.

After the guys had left, I looked back up at him. He was pulling a one-hitter weed pipe out of his backpack and took a hit. He saw me staring at him and smiled, put the one hitter away, and took a hat out of his backpack that read: CIA. He put it on, walked down the bleachers, and casually sat down next to me. The sun was still somewhat warm as the wind began to blow. It would be cold out soon enough.

"What's your name?" he asked me, smiling like he knew a secret that he might just let me in on.

"Jackson."

"Well, Jackson, do you get high?"

"No, not really."

"That's probably why you have such a lame backpack."

I was kind of shocked by his blunt comment and looked down at my backpack, sadly resting between my feet. My mom had bought it for me at K-Mart. It was bright blue, with a leather brand tag sewn on it. His was all black and covered in band patches like, *Black Flag, Suicidal Tendencies* and *Dead Kennedys*. He saw me looking at my backpack self-consciously.

"Don't worry about that. We can burn it," he said half-seriously. "Jackson. Can I ask you a serious question?" I braced myself for a devastating epithet, figuring he'd ask me something like, *Do you play with dolls?* "Do you believe in the existence of the Sasquatch?" He looked at me intently, like there was a lot riding on my answer. It caught me so off guard that I laughed longer and louder than I'd laughed in a while.

I finished the beer and walked outside the bar and just wandered down the road in the dark trying to sober up for the drive back to the motel and what awaited me there. There was a sliver of a moon, and the wind blew right through me as I tried to feel something, anything other than being sick to my stomach as a wave of panic filled me and I realized I was in real trouble.

6.

The next day I drove into San Francisco and was uncomfortable in the one place where I always felt so good as a child. I went to Golden Gate Park under a sheet of fog and walked the nearby streets of Haight Ashbury that I was so in awe of as a kid—back then, in awe that all of life could be, full of anticipation and excitement, and just *content* to be alive. Now, I wandered the same concrete streets searching for that childhood euphoria. Instead, I found myself on the Golden Gate Bridge, the wind howling as cars blasted by oblivious of me gazing into the fading sun through the mist. I looked down at the bay's cresting waves of freezing water, imagining the feeling of my feet leaving the rust-colored railing and plunging downward. Scared of myself and my mindset and what was happening to me, I turned and walked hurriedly toward the park and the safety of land. I lay in the grass under the shelter of a tree until the storm in my mind subsided.

I went back to my car and drove across the Bay Bridge toward my grandparent's house in the hills above Oakland. I stopped at the elementary school down the street from their house where grandma took me to play when I was a kid, pushing me on the swings. I tried to recapture that feeling of safety, comfort, and simple bliss as it started to rain. I was just here eight months ago visiting for Christmas. I bought a jade necklace for Caitlin in Chinatown that she liked. I wanted to call her and tell her that I was sorry and hoped that she missed me, and that everything would be okay and hear her say that everything would be okay and that I should come back to Salt Lake City.

I drove through the glistening wet streets to a gas station down the street near Lake Merritt, walked up to a pay phone but couldn't bring myself to call her. I didn't want her to know how broken I was. I banged the phone on the phone box, angry at not knowing what to do. I called my grandparents.

"Are you okay, son?" my grandma asked me tenderly, and I suddenly felt a lump in my throat.

"I'm fine grandma," I lied. "I won't be coming to stay for a couple more days. I've made some other plans and am going to visit a friend."

"Okay, dear. Are you sure you're okay?"

"I'm fine grandma. I can't wait to see you and grandpa. Maybe for Sunday dinner," I said, half-believing it myself.

"Okay, Jackson. We look forward to seeing you too. You take your time. Have fun with your friend. We'll be here."

I felt like an asshole for lying to her, the kindest sweetest person I've ever known. I drove back to San Francisco in a daze.

I checked into another cheap motel out by the airport. Mom's money was almost gone. For a couple of days, I wandered the streets, drinking my way through strip clubs and dive bars, past the strung-out rent boys selling themselves in the dark halls of the sex shops, fidgeting with the doorknobs of the female porn booths, with the smell of cum on the floors, just to take a peak. The women in the strip clubs moved themselves vacantly on stage, transfixed by their reflections in the mirrors that lined the walls, searching for clues

about themselves, just like me. But I couldn't stop thinking about

ending it all. I could feel a *dark presence* closing in on me

everywhere I went so I headed back to the motel.

 "This is a bad idea," Aaron said, as I looked out the room's

rain-streaked window at the passing cars on the freeway, drinking

whiskey from the bottle. I didn't want to hear him and tuned him

out. I watched the sun, as if for the last time, slowly setting with a

dreamlike quality in the haze. Soon the alcohol was gone; the night

and its darkness had fallen, and outside the winds were blowing

strong. Later I walked out of the room into the night. The hallway

swayed as cold sweat dripped off my face under the flickering lights.

The *demons*. A woman in the hallway instinctively pulled her

daughter away from me. The little girl said as I passed by them,

"Mommy, what's wrong with him?"

 "I don't know honey, but he doesn't look well."

 I didn't know either, I thought.

 I huddled against the cold as I walked through the near-

deserted streets, the alcohol racing through my veins and pushing me

along. Homeless people stumbled out of my way, recognizing the crazed look in my eyes as I strode hurriedly across the litter-strewn sidewalk toward the pale light of a corner convenience store. I grabbed a pack of razor blades, some whisky and champagne, and put them on the counter under the deathly green fluorescent lights, flickering knowingly. Those damn demons.

"Celebrating, huh," the ashen-faced old man behind the bulletproof plexiglass window asked.

"Yeah, life. Ain't it just grand?"

"Nothin' better out there, bud," he said dryly. Did he wonder what the razor blades were for, or would have cared less if I was going to off myself? He didn't ask for ID.

"Yep, fucking grand!" I said with a sarcastic sneer.

Back in the room I thought about writing a note to Mom, as I stared out the window at the lights of the passing cars searching for a way through the fog. I got a pen and paper, sat down at the table and opened the champagne. It started spewing all over the table. I wiped it off with the cuff of my shirt, then grabbed the bottle and started guzzling it down in long gulps until half of the bottle was gone. I then wrote: "Life! I tried, but it's a pretty sorry mess . . . Sorry."

Shit. That was all I could come up with, and I ripped the note to pieces.

It all just seems surreal, looking back now, like it wasn't even me, like I'm watching a movie about a sad twin brother no one told me about. After that it just got kind of blurry. I remembered that I wanted to call Caitlin again, but my thoughts were racing and I was pacing the room, and instead of calling her, I ended up calling a girl from an escort ad at the back of one of those shitty sex mags I'd picked up off the street. I vaguely remember sitting on the floor of the motel room thinking I'd talked to Caitlin and told her how I felt, when the girl knocked on the door. She looked nothing like Caitlin, but she was okay with me calling her that, which I thought was nice of her even though she couldn't even pretend that she cared. She wouldn't let me kiss her though, which we discussed for a long time and by the time we sorted that out, I didn't even want to have sex but did, because she expected it, since I'd already paid her. I had trouble getting off which was embarrassing, but she was nice about it and patient with me, kind of like you'd hope a real girlfriend would be, which just made it all more miserable because I was paying her.

After she left, I don't really remember much. I just wanted to end it all, despite Aaron trying to coax me out of it. But I just didn't do a very good job of it. I was too drunk, I guess. When I woke up, sick in the tub covered in vomit and blood from my cut wrist, all I could hear was Aaron's voice saying, "Call 911, Bro! Call 911!"

Later, in my sleep, I could hear someone crying, which slowly woke me. They sounded pitiful, like a wounded animal. I felt sorry for them. The halcyon-white and cold-steel room slowly took shape as I felt the hot tears streaming down my face. I soon realized that I was the one who had been crying. My arms and legs were strapped to a gurney. I was wearing a hospital gown and hooked up to an I.V. and lay there alone in the dark. A young nurse came into my curtained-off area, turned on an overhead light. I tried to move my arm out of the restraints to wipe my face as I didn't want her to see that I had been crying, but it was no use.

"It's okay," she said, putting her hand on my forehead. "You're fine now." The nurse had striking blue eyes framed by golden hair and a brilliant, white smile. She looked over my chart.

"Do you know where you are?" I shook my head. "You're in the ER. You tried to kill yourself and almost needed a blood transfusion. You came close to dying. I'm sorry for the restraints. You'll just be strapped down until they move you to the ICU." I tried to speak, but my mouth was too dry and no words came out. She looked at me with a mixture of pity and empathy, and then said, "I don't know what's so wrong in your life that you would do this to yourself, but I'm sorry and it may not seem like it now, but everything will be okay." Why did people keep saying that? Did they know something I didn't?

I don't know what's wrong with me either, I tried to say, but no words came, and I fell back to sleep, back into the darkness.

Later on, I woke up sweating and soaking the sheets as I slowly started to come around, paralyzed in the darkness of the hospital room. I could see the dark presence standing over me, and I tried to scream but nothing came out. Over and over again, I screamed soundlessly into the emptiness.

The next day, I was lying strapped to a gurney in a waiting room, waiting to be sent to the Intensive Care Unit, stretched out as if the soul that filled my body with life was absent. I didn't know what was happening to me anymore, like I'd just gone so completely far off the rails that I wasn't really alive. No one had ever told me about the possibility of something like this happening, especially not growing up when everyone was so convinced that I was special. It was all just completely unreal, as if it were happening to someone else. A weathered old police officer, who stood by the door of the ER, looked over at me as though he felt my pain and said, "You need some help, buddy?"

"Yeah . . ." was all I could manage before looking away, embarrassed to have to admit that to myself and to a total stranger.

"Don't worry. They'll fix ya up here," he said, with his clipped San Francisco cop accent. He smiled earnestly like this wasn't his first suicide case, "They'll take care of ya, believe me." But do I really want to be "taken care of," I thought to myself.

PART II

7.

A large, muscular male nurse pushes me through the hospital to the Intensive Care Unit, or ICU, as they call it. As he strolls me down the hall, a certain relief comes over me knowing I won't have to make any more decisions for myself, or at least for a while.

"You doin' alright, my man?" the nurse asks.

"Yeah, I'm fine," I say. "This is nice."

"Okay, my man. That's the spirit."

When we get to the ICU, the nurse presses a call button next to two large doors with small round thick-glass windows like on a ship. I picture a crazy gang of pirates on the other side of the door eagerly awaiting their next hostage.

The speaker next to the door crackles. "You got Jackson Smith out there?"

"Yes, ma'am. Checking him into the luxury suite." He winks at me.

"Okay." The woman on the intercom laughs. "He's gonna be real disappointed. All our suites are gone." They both laugh.

We hear the sounds of a commotion on the other side of the doors, then some shouting. Someone says, "We need you to calm down."

The speaker crackles on again. "Can you give us a minute, Marcus? Got a situation in here."

Marcus pushes the call button. "Copy that." A looming sense of dread creeps over me.

"It ain't that bad in there, man. Don't worry," Marcus says, sensing my growing unease.

"You can all die!" yells a woman on the other side of the doors. "You can all go to hell!"

"Okay, so here's the drill," Marcus says to me, ignoring the commotion. "Before we get in there, I need to know that you're not going to try to harm yourself or anyone else." He looks at me seriously, and I nod my head. "I need a verbal confirmation."

"I'm not going to hurt myself or anyone else," I say. "I promise, really." Marcus smiles.

The intercom crackles. "You're clear to bring in Mr. Jackson."

"Okay my man, it's time for your big entrance. Let's do this."

Marcus wheels me into the ward. There's a long hall with dorm-type rooms on the right side, and exam rooms and a nurses' station, surrounded by thick plexiglass and what looks like the command room for a confused pirate ship, on the left. Here sits what looks to be a prisoner taken by the pirates, or an old woman accused of mutiny. Her hair is a shock of white shooting out in all directions.

She has tired, loose and sagging skin, but her eyes are black infernos of pent-up rage. She is strapped to the chair with Velcro restraints. She yells at me, "You go to hell!"

"Okay! That's enough!" One of the nurses yells out to her.

"You go to hell too!"

"Got it." The nurse says, somewhat resigned. The old woman looks down at the floor like she's suddenly tired. Everyone else is in their rooms sleeping or maybe planning ways to escape. The place smells like the nursing home my paternal grandpa lived in before he died.

Marcus wheels me up to the nurses' command station. "I'm going to take Mr. Jackson here to one of the rooms and go over the orientation with him."

"Okay." One of the three nurses behind the command station says, "Room 3 is open."

"You think you can get up, my man, without falling over?"

"Yeah, I'm fine," I say.

"All right then. Let's go to room 3." The nurse hands him a folder.

The small room has white walls, a white table and chairs under fluorescent lights. The folder sits on the table between us. I'm a little cold in my hospital scrubs, extremely tired, and hungry.

Marcus picks up the folder. "Okay, Jackson. I'm going to get you through this as quickly as possible as you're probably tired. Right?" I nod my head.

"Before we get started, I want you to know that I was once in your shoes a little over fifteen years ago, and I know how bleak things can look when your life takes this turn. But I also want you to know that things can get better. And don't feel bad about trying to take your life, or for being here." I nod my head as I fight back tears. "You're going to get through this." He pauses and looks at me square in the eyes. "And you're going to be a better human being for going through it. Believe me, Jackson. Okay?"

"Okay."

"Now here's what you can expect. There's group therapy sessions three times a day. They're not mandatory, but they're suggested. In some of them you get to do things like painting or working with clay. Breakfast is at 7:00, lunch at noon, and dinner at

6:00. Visitors can come on Saturday or Sunday, but I believe you're on your own out here in San Francisco. Is that right?"

"Yeah. My grandparents live in Oakland but are too old to drive. My parents live in Utah."

"Well, your parents have been notified about what's happened and know that you're all right. I think they're planning on coming to see you." My stomach starts to turn at the thought of them coming here. "That's pretty much it as far as how the ward runs. Obviously, there's no fighting, and if you feel threatened by anyone just let one of the staff members know. Okay?" I nod my head, feeling sleepy. "Also, after you lie down for a bit, you'll have the intake with the psych doctor, then twice weekly sessions with the psychiatrist assigned to you. Okay, Jackson. Does all this make sense?" I nod my head. My eyes are heavy, and my body feels full of lead.

"Let's get you to your bed."

A week later it's now time for another group therapy session in the ICU. It's starting to get dark outside. Someone down the hall is yelling, "Fucking die! Die fucking die!" from one of the rooms.

We are gathered in the eating/sitting/television/meeting room, while the cleaning lady mops the linoleum floor. Koran stands up and wants the mop thinking that she can do a better job.

"Can I have the mop please?" she asks the heavyset, kind-looking woman in the faded -white uniform.

"I wouldn't mind dear, but it's my job," the cleaning lady says in a motherly tone. Koran is pretty but worn down from too much life. There's lots of pain in her eyes. But she still manages to smile somehow, anyhow. She seems full of an inner light that I remember once having too when I was young. Koran now stands by the cleaning lady, watching and pointing out dirty spots to her, as she goes along to make sure the woman doesn't miss anything. Then Koran walks around the room tidying things up and talking to herself and anyone else nearby.

Seeing Koran smile, given her pain, I try to convince myself that living is worth the suffering, that it does get better. I want to believe that, try to convince myself that everything will be fine, that things aren't really as bad as I've made them out to be, convince myself that I'm really not that broken. But I am. This place is proof of it. I feel *that*, even if the staff doctors tell me that my mental illness is just a preliminary stage to my eventual cure, a stage in my evolving life and that now I'm getting better.

"Don't miss that spot," Koran says coming back to the cleaning lady and pointing out a smudge near my feet, gently pulling me out of my thoughts. I'm staring out the windows to the darkening sky over the city of San Francisco as the therapist leading the group rambles on in the background about hope.

"Koran, can you come back to group please?" the therapist pleads.

"Okay. I'm sorry. I was just helpin' out," Koran replies in her mile-a-minute way of talking.

"Thank you for your help, dear," the cleaning lady says as Koran sits back down.

"Life didn't make sense to me," one of the patients continues, "I couldn't figure out what was happening to me and I gave in. Now this is where I belong."

"Koran," the therapist says, "what do you think about that?"

"If we don't have no hope that things are gonna get better," Koran says, "then there's no point in livin'."

"Thank you, Koran. Do you have hope?" she prods.

"I'm tryin', but it can be a pretty nasty, mean old world out there that don't care about your feelins'!" she says and laughs. The therapist frowns, and I can't help but smile.

After group therapy, Koran tells the cleaning lady that she did a good job.

The woman smiles. "Bless you dear," she says.

The intercom now crackles, "Snack time . . . Make sure to *crackle, crackle, crackle.*"

I'm tired and I just want to be alone and go back to my room. I lie down on the bed and stare out the window at night. My roommate asks, "Time! Time! What time is it?!" I calmly tell him that it's a little after 9 o'clock.

"AM or PM?!" he yells.

"PM," I tell him, flatly.

I now hear another commentary from Aaron. "*Jesus. This is what's gonna happen to you if you don't get yourself together! You're not gonna know whether it's am or pm, and they definitely won't let you out if you don't even know that much. SO, get yourself some rest and some snacks, and get ready to get yourself back out there in the real world! This is no good for you. I know you've been having some alien demonic experiences ever since we did all that*

acid down in Southern Utah, but you also had a God moment. And

that's the tradeoff. You can't have one without the other. That's just

the way it is. You've just got to pay attention to the light and not give

a shit about the darkness. The reason the darkness is messing with

you so bad right now is that they know you saw the light! Don't pay

no attention to those demons and the darkness!"

I laugh at this tirade, even if it sounds familiar.

"What's funny?" my roommate asks.

"Nothing, just my friend going off about things."

"Okay," he says, as if talking to spirits is par for the course. "Are you sure it's still night?" I look out the window. It's still night time.

"Yes, and I say that with 90 percent assurance," I tell him, mimicking Bill Murray in *Groundhog Day*. "It's still night."

"Okay, thanks roommate."

"You're welcome." He now turns over and goes back to sleep.

Aaron's right. I've got to get myself back together and out of this place, or I'll become this guy for sure.

I lie in bed for a while, the muffled voices from the nurse's station drifting down the hall. Unable to sleep, I think about when Aaron and I got home from the desert after dropping acid, that night I woke to terrifyingly, dark, malevolent *entities* standing over me in my room. Two shadowy figures were whispering to each other, seemingly about my warped fate. I tried to scream with all my will, but nothing came out. I struggled to throw my covers off, jump up, and wrack them, but I was completely frozen and powerless to move. My eyes darted around the room; the clock read 3 am. Suddenly, the bed began to open up beneath me revealing a fiery hellish pit of infinite torment. There, a mountain of ghoulish, rotting, and decaying creatures screeched, gnashed, and cried out ripping each other from limb to limb trying to reach me as I slowly sank down closer and closer to them and this infinite inferno. I could feel the heat, smell the stench, and feel their agony as I tried to scream again and again until they were about to reach me. In desperation I did the only thing I could think of, and I prayed for the first time in my life, *God please help me!* Suddenly, I shot straight up out of my body through the roof and into the night sky where I hovered quietly above the quiet tree-lined streets of the neighborhood below. I felt so at peace that I never wanted to return to my body, and as *soon* as I

had that thought, I shot back down into my room and into my body,

filled with an *immense* terror. I jumped out of bed flipping on the

lights and expecting to see those two ghoulish entities in my room,

but I was alone.

I didn't speak to anyone about this terrifying experience,

actually about anything at all for the next couple of days as I was

trying to figure out what had happened, until I finally told Aaron.

His eyes got big and wide when I told him, and he smiled, "Ah,

don't be afraid of them!" he said, laughing. "They're just little shits!

Parasites! Like gnats on an elephant! Tell them to bring it on. We

can take them. No problem. They messed with the wrong guys."

"Lights out, " the intercom says, screeches, then crackles into

silence, and I fade off into sleep.

8.

I feel safe here in the hospital, cut off from the outside, and tucked

away. There are six rooms on this ward with twelve beds. The doors

of our rooms are left open at night, and the light and voices from the

nurse's station float softly down the hall. My roommate snores and I look over at him. He's big and overweight, sad and broken. He spends most of his time in bed. Tonight, after dinner I brought him a carton of milk. We're not supposed to take food out of the eating area. The nurses told me that they don't want me to cater to my roommate; they want him to learn how to take care of himself. I think that he just needs someone who seems to give a damn about him. I asked the nurses about him, how he got this way, but of course they won't share a patient's history. So, I took him something to drink. I don't think that he has anyone in the entire world. He seems to be sleeping soundly tonight, but he now rolls over and asks me again what time it is, then asks, "am or pm?" I tell him, pm, and then he goes back to sleep.

But then I wonder, am I any better? I mean, I have nowhere else to go either. And I feel alone. I settle into my bed.

As I drift off to sleep, the shadowy presence stands at the foot of the bed. I'm paralyzed by fear, and I scream for help in vain into the emptiness inside of me. Is anybody there?

I wake up the next day. The sun is shining. I get dressed and walk down to breakfast. Everybody looks like zombies. Bad night?

Afterward, we head off to Group Therapy. After a while, my turn

comes. I share doubts about my sanity.

"*You're* not crazy; you're just sad, a little lost and confused,"

says the perky, optimistic therapist in front of everyone. So now

they're all staring at me, looking like a disoriented, dazed and

broken band of soul soldiers searching for evidence of a miracle or

an alien landing. It's like they want me to say something

encouraging, but this is all so surreal that I've swallowed my words

and my head nods involuntarily. I look out the windows at the sun

that momentarily blinds me, and I picture Aaron, with his wild eyes

and unruly hair, riding a giant buffalo in sky (he was half Indian—a

Choctaw like his mom) holding a spear and pointing to a path in the

sky, our shared destiny. And I start laughing at the image so hard

that I can't catch my breath, and I put my head in my hands as the

therapist asks me, "Jackson, are you all right?"

I nod my head yes and try to contain my laughter because it

probably looks like I'm really crazy, but it's such a funny image of

Aaron riding a buffalo in the sky leading us all out of the hospital to

our salvations or at least to the next watering hole. I just can't stop

laughing with my head between my arms folded over almost

between my legs. The tears keep coming to my eyes, and Koran starts laughing her great laugh like she can see the image in my mind or at least *gets* somehow why I'm laughing and says, "Jackson, I love you. You crazy!"

"What are you laughing about Jackson?" asks the therapist warmly and earnestly.

"My dead friend," I say looking up smiling and leaving it at that. I try to stop laughing, wiping tears from my eyes, looking around at the dazed and confused looks of the other patients, and then suddenly feeling really sad for some reason. I mean, if I shared my vision, they'd probably start force feeding me the drugs.

"I'm very sorry about your friend, but *you're* going to make some new friends, Jackson," the therapist says, looking around the group to see if there are any takers, pleading with her eyes for somebody to say something. Koran picks up on the cue, as I lean forward perching my head onto my fists as though I'm thinking about something. She puts her hand on my back and says, "I'm your friend Jackson" And I start beaming like I'm eight years old and new at school, and I just made my first friend.

"Really," I ask. Koran just flashes that great smile again.

Sitting in my room after group and looking out the window at the sun slowly being swallowed by the fog, with my roommate sleeping and lost in his own fog, it feels like life might just be some shitty test or something to see how much pain we can take without breaking or going wacky. They keep saying in here that God has a plan for you, but it seems to me that the only real plan he's got is to watch people crumble under the weight of the world, and then ask them if they need a hand up. Kinda lame if you ask me; I mean, he's created us to just keep giving us pain until we either snap, let our hearts turn dark, or turn to him. Seems kinda like a rigged system to me. Just then my roommate moans in his sleep like he's being terrorized by something, and he tosses and turns for a minute, then goes back to snoring. I think about my own night demons and wonder about telling my doctor or a priest or somebody about them.

On cue, I hear Aaron say, "*If you tell people about them right now, they're just going to think that you're really crazy. They'll ask you about when they first came to visit you, and you'll tell them about all the acid we did down in the desert just before that, and they'll totally discount your experience as being a drug after-effect. We both know they're real. You had a God experience down there in the desert buddy, and the Devil sensed it, and now he's sent his henchmen after you to try and make you go crazy and kill yourself. But we're gonna get you out of this! So, let's focus on your recovery, okay?"*

I nod my head as my roommate thrashes about and mumbles, "Don't kill me."

Why didn't someone tell us that demons were a possible side effect of taking acid?

"I'm sure someone did. Now pay attention. This is serious."

I am paying attention.

"Okay, then pay more attention."

I nod to myself. My roommate grumbles, as if he's listening in. Maybe I am crazy?

"Pay attention!"

Okay, okay. I got it.

"If there's demons on your ass, then you just might have some angels too . . . Hell, I might be one! So, let's just go with that for now, and we'll figure out the rest of this as we go along. Okay buddy?"

Okay, I say nodding my head, and my roommate growls like he's possessed by one of those demons who doesn't like this plan.

"It's smoke break and free time," the intercom crackles like this signal is coming from outer space.

I stand up and walk down the hall as if answering this summons. The smokers are all outside in the walled-in terrace with concrete benches and potted plants, sitting in the light of what's left of the fog-engulfed sun. It's like mayhem out there. They're all talking loud and waving their hands in the air, pointing at the sky and smoking like banshees. The walls are too high to climb so they're unattended and free to smoke and freak out when it's nice out. I've only been here a little while, but the sky and the outside or real world seems like a dream or a bad memory that I don't want to revisit. I think maybe that's what people mean when they say someone's been institutionalized. I don't have any smokes, and I don't want to ask anyone for a cig since I'd have to talk to them, and I really just feel like I want to be left alone. So, I sit on a bench and watch them, their arms waving wildly through the plumes of smoke, as I wonder why the thought of going outside and being in the world makes me so terribly uncomfortable.

"Jackson," one of the nurses calls out, "the doctor wants to see you in her office."

"Okay." This will be my first session with her.

9.

Dr. Canter looks serious and sensitive and rather young in her professional tweed outfit, sensible glasses, and functional shoes. After going over my chart and nodding her head seriously, she reviews my whole story again with me, and then says, "I think your issues have been building for a while, and they just culminated and came to a head with the death of your friend. So, tell me, what do you want to do with your life, Jackson?"

I think about this question for a long moment searching my brain for any answers, and I realize she's pretty much nailed me. I start sweating a little bit and get a rather red in the face because I don't have the slightest fucking idea about "what I want to do with my life." I'm getting more flustered; honestly, right now, it all seems like a big giant fucking joke to me. I just say the first thing that comes to mind and then realize that I'm sounding crazy as I ramble on, but I don't really give a shit. I just *don't know* anything anymore!

I say, "I guess get a job, tune out and turn off, become a cog in the machine, get cancer and quietly suffer until the day I die?" I wave my hands in the air as I finish to emphasize my point.

She smiles at this lame rendering of modern life. "Is that how life looks to you? That boring and uninteresting?"

"Yeah, pretty much," I say, looking around the room and noticing a dream catcher on the wall above a picture of an Indian on his galloping horse leaning back with his head and arms spread wide toward the sky. Wow. It reminds me of the image I had of Aaron riding the Great Buffalo in the sky. That's something.

"Anything else?" she asks.

I look back at her, "Maybe get married. Have a kid. Get divorced. Pay alimony and child support until I'm a dry husk of a human," I say, and then add, "Oh, or maybe become a hermit and write Zen poems." I remember reading about these Chinese hermit poets from centuries ago who were all thought to be crazy. I feel like I could really do this line of work.

She smiles at this last remark. "And how would you make money?"

"See, that's the whole problem. Money!" I throw my hands up like I'm throwing a wad of money up in the air. "Money is the invisible hand that makes everyone dance like a monkey in a suit on the street corner to an out of tune organ grinder."

"That's an interesting analogy. You've been thinking about this for a while?"

"Yes," I say, calming down as I settle back into the couch. "I'd also like to be a good person, but that doesn't seem to pay very well. Just look at the nurses out there on the ward."

She nods and looks at me with a sympathetic look of understanding, then says flatly, "I want to start you on some medication."

"Oh yeah, I forgot about that part. I want to be on medication too."

She raises her eyebrows at me. I guess I look seriously off to her. "We'll talk again tomorrow. That's all for today. I'll let your parents know how you're doing. Try and get some rest."

"Okay. How long do you think I'll be here?"

"Just try to relax and get comfortable and see this as a break from life to get well again and settle back in."

I nod. It's not like I've got anywhere to go in my shape.

"Things are going to be okay," she says as I stand up and leave the room.

The doc has control of my life now because I couldn't control it. I feel bad about my feeble responses. She's just trying to help. Also, I feel like I should be doing something to get myself out of here as I walk down the hall and head back to my room to think of a way out of this mess. I don't want to be in this maniac haven. I can't take this insanity. People are mumbling to themselves, mumbling to the television set as the skinny, sketchy-looking girl named Shelly yells at the nurses, "Come and help him! Come and help him! He's pissing himself again!" I look over into the television/eating/sitting/group room. The old Polish man with no teeth is standing in front of the television pissing his pants, his pee pooling on the floor. Being here just suddenly seems so terribly wrong and strange that it couldn't be true, but it is. The old Polish guy is laughing and yells, "Shit! Shit! I Shit!" And the nurses come rushing over and start to guide him back to his room before he shits on the floor. I just shake my head and desperately want to go home.

"Smoke time is over!" Marcus, the big male nurse, yells out the cracked-open sliding glass door into the fog of smoke that looks like it's captured our helpless patients. All the smokers come piling back inside stinking of cigarettes. He locks the door behind them. The long fluorescent tube light flickers overhead, buzzing and seeming to sap the energy right out of me as the other patients mumble and jabber to themselves and treat each other like overgrown kids at recess.

"Recreation time!" Marcus yells, his girth blocking out light from the sliding glass doors.

The therapist this morning said that life is what you make of it and I've made my life pretty crazy, but I'm not going to settle for that. Am I?

As I pass Marcus, he sticks out his hand to do a fist bump. "How's it goin', my man?"

"Couldn't be better, Marcus," I ly. He scrunches his face, not believing me.

I somehow made it through a couple more nights, and this morning I took my third dose of the antidepressant they prescribed, and so now

Dr. Canter wants to see how I feel. Her office is filled with thick colorful rugs, black-and-white framed photographs, the windows look out toward the city shrouded in fog. She sits behind a large wooden desk looking very stern in a different tweed outfit, but the same serious glasses and sensible shoes.

"Sit down, Jackson," she says.

"Careful what you say. No more, off the rails, rants like the other day! Just try to stay focused on getting out of here!" Aaron tells me, and I nod my head obediently, then stop, realizing that doing that probably makes me look crazy.

I sit on the large sofa across from her. She scans me from her leather chair, like she's the captain of the *Starship Enterprise* and I'm a captive Klingon.

"So, tell me, how do you feel on the new medication?"

"Well, it's like my brain has been jump-started by a lawnmower."

She crinkles her nose and squints, staring at me as if I had just passed gas.

"That's a good thing," she says, deciding to go with my reply. She now earnestly asks, "So, tell me, how did you end up here?

Despite Aaron's warning, I just start rambling on. "Well I don't know how I ended up here. I think I was just tired of feeling like I didn't belong anywhere anymore, that I didn't really have anywhere to go and that I'd become like a burden to everyone. Guess I was feeling pretty sad and lonely after breaking up with my girlfriend. But then she wasn't a real girlfriend since she wouldn't talk to me in public, only let me make out with her when we were alone. I don't know; it's all kinda fuzzy."

The doctor nods her head understandingly, and I go on for what seems like an hour or more. I completely spill my guts. It must be the drug. I don't even know what I'm talking about, but my arms are moving animatedly and then I'm getting angry and soon I'm crying. And she just keeps on nodding knowingly, smiles and says, "I understand," a lot. When I'm done, she takes a deep breath then says, "I think you're in the right place, Jackson. You've been severely depressed. And the hope is, with the medication, that it may help clear the dark filter of your depression and help you to see things more clearly again."

"Okay, I'm all for that," I say, nodding my head and staring off into space. I think that she's made a pretty decent point. Things have been going poorly lately. Maybe the meds will help.

"So, let's have you settle in and take it easy for a little bit. Things seem bleak right now, but with some help and some work that will pass."

I nod my head, stand up, and go back to my room to reflect on things like the doctor suggests. My roommate is sleeping. No change there. The room is still and heavy, and kinda dark. I lie on the stiff mattress staring through the small, dirty window to the heavy dismal fog outside and think of Prozac. And wonder what if the window to my soul is dirty, maybe Prozac can clean it? Then what, if it's still dark and dismal outside?

10.

We play hangman for group therapy tonight in the eating/sitting/break/television room. One of the patients with ecstatic hair and eager eyes draws stick figures on the chalkboard as we try to guess the letters to the unknown word and its therapeutic value under the blaring fluorescent lights. I look around the room filled with tired green sofas, flimsy tables, and dilapidated chairs. I'm crushed by the weight of sadness and sigh as the young therapist in a khaki skirt yells enthusiastically, "We have a winner!" The guy at the chalkboard jumps up and down squinting his face like a kid whose deepest secret has just been revealed.

Koran jumps to her feet smiling, raising her arms in victory. "JOYFULNESS," she yells!

"Yes Koran," the therapist waves her hands animatedly! "Joyfulness!"

"I knew I was gonna get it!" Koran says. "I was about to say it; it was on the tip of my damn tongue, then I jus' yelled it. I knew it was gonna be something to do with happiness, because we all need more happiness? Right!"

"Yes, we do Koran," the therapist says, looking around the room. "How many of you could use more happiness?"

Koran and I and the guy at the chalkboard are the only ones who raise our hands. No one else seems to give a crap about joyfulness.

"Come on now," Koran says. "I know y'all ain't that happy!"

The wild-looking guy at the board with his boxers hanging out jumps up and down smiling animatedly.

"I could use a smoke," someone says.

"After group," the therapist replies with a frown.

I love the way everything with Koran comes out all at once. She gets so excited that it's like she can't contain herself. I smile at her in awe. She's the first person in a while to catch my attention, the first person that I've seen in, I can't remember how long, that really seems *alive*. When I first saw her, I thought she was a lot younger. She looks and acts so young, almost childlike. But under the bright lights I can see the years worn deep into her face. Her eyes shine brighter than any I've ever seen. They have a spark of life in them that's so contagious that I can't help but smile. I want to get to know her better. I'd like to hear about how she got here.

"Koran," says the therapist, holding up two cans of soda, "for being the winner of hangman tonight, you get a Coke and Sprite."

Koran claps her hands and says, "Ohhh," like she just won a gold medal and takes the soda cans. Then she gives the skinny girl, Shelly, with ratty hair and a suspicious look in her eyes, the Sprite and hands me the Coke. "Because y'all are new," she says. I pour half of my Coke in a cup and give it to a guy named Ahmad; he looks like he needs the sugar surge much more than I do. He's Middle Eastern and short and reminds me of a disgruntled Buddha. His grey-black hair stands up scattered about three inches off his head, his pants sag and drag on the floor, and his stomach hangs out from under his shirt. Most of the time he's shuffling around the ward with his eyes rolled up toward the top of his head so that all you can see are the whites staring blankly back at you as he mumbles, "I smoke! I smoke! I smoke!" Whenever he walks by me, he steals a glimpse at the cut on my wrist. His eyes roll down from the top of his head as I hand him the Coke in a plastic cup. He steals another glimpse of my wrist, mumbles, "Thank you," then takes another look at my scar. I notice that his shirt sleeves are pulled down to cover his wrists.

After the game I'm writing on a notepad on one of the puke-green sofas as everyone else watches television. A big guy named Steven who's about thirty sits down next to me. He's as tall as me, over 6 foot, but outweighs me by 30 or 40 pounds.

"Are you writing a book?"

"No. I'm just writing because the doctor says it would be therapeutic for me."

"How's that working for you?" he asks seriously.

"Okay, I guess."

"You should think of writing it as a book. Stories of mental crack-ups and recoveries are big these days," he says with some authority. It appears he's researched the subject. He smiles at me. "I thought about writing my own testament down," he says. "I'm a Christian Catholic-Protestant. A big audience. Did you know that the first memoir ever written was by Saint Augustus?" He shakes his head like he's mad at himself. "St. Augustine, I mean, give me a break."

"No. I didn't know that."

"Memoirs are a big thing now Jackson. Take *Prozac Nation* for instance. That's a really big book. I just read it. It's a memoir about a young girl's depression and the overmedication of our society. Are you on medication?"

I nod my head, feeling a burning sensation in my gut. "I just started taking Prozac."

"Oh, that's not good. That's how they get you hooked. They started me on Prozac. Now they've got me on all kinds of medications: Lithium, Trazodone, Buspar, Seroquel . . . Did you check yourself in here?"

"I guess the paramedics did."

"Did you try to kill yourself?"

"I cut my wrist, but not very good." He looks at my wrist, nods his head then looks away.
"I've thought about that too."

Since we are being honest with each other, I asked, "Why are you here?"

He squints his eyes suspiciously, like I'm an undercover agent working for the government. I smile. "I threatened some people I didn't like. Let's leave it at that."

I nod my head. He now looks back at the old woman with scraggly hair behind us at one of the tables whose been preaching to herself about religion as Steven and I talk.

"I'm a Christian and an Atheist Buddhist," she says.

"Amy," Steven says, glaring at her, "go away; we're talking."

"I'm a Wiccan Buddhist," Amy says. "What are you guys?"

"Nothing Amy! Mind your own business." Steven now turns to me. "She just wants attention."

"Catholic, Wican Templar of the Roundtable," she says and gets up and wanders off.

Steven looks intensely at me. "I think that God could do a lot for you Jackson," he says in his kind of droning voice as he stands up. "I gotta call my Ma and apologize. I may have threatened her last time we talked." He walks over to one of the three phone booths along the wall pulling his pants up as he walks, steps into one of the booths, and picks up the phone. He's too big to fit all the way in the booth and shut the door. His legs and his belly spilling out.

"Ma, Ma," he says. I needa tell you something. I'm sorry about our last talk. I really didn't mean it." There's a long pause as his mother responds. "I'm moving to the YMCA, Ma when I get out . . . *Yeah* I *know*, Ma! But I need my freedom! I'm going to take my own medication and everything. I'm going to take swimming lessons, craft lessons, lift weights, and calm my mind . . . Okay Ma, we'll talk about it later. I'm converting a guy right now named Jackson, Ma . . . Yeah, I know Ma, but he needs *something*."

When he gets off the phone, he walks over to me and says, *"Recovery in the Mental Ward*. I think that would be a good title for your book." I wonder if he expects a cut. He nods his head to himself then wanders off.

A few minutes later Steven comes back over, sits down next to me, and says he's found the meaning of life as I continue to write and stare out the window at the great expanse of the San Francisco night.

"You might want to write it down, Jackson . . . I mean, the fucking meaning of life," he says, as his gaze drags across the linoleum floor and then to my notebook.

"Okay, let's hear it," I tell him. He looks as though he's thinking about it or maybe he's just stoned from too much medication. He stands up absentmindedly, walks toward the hallway, and I trail along.

"The search has ended," he says as we walk down the tired and worn-out brown carpeted hallway. "I tried New Age Philosophy. That didn't work. I tried Catholicism. That didn't work. Then I tried being a Christian Catholic-Protestant . . ." He trails off after one trip down the hall, and I follow him into the group room where he sits down on one of the green couches, begins rocking back and forth, rubbing his balding head and his stomach, drooling a little, but he's smiling. He stares off into space and doesn't finish his thought. I sit down next to him.

"Are you high, Steven," I ask?

"Why? Do I look like it," he asks, as his eyes roll toward me from wherever they were lost just a second ago. He looks at me, trying to find me it seems through his thick glasses, still drooling a bit, but smiling, rocking back and forth, and rubbing his Buddha stomach again. I wonder if he's going to spit out coins.

"Yeah, you look a little high," I tell him. He nods his head with his eyes closed, then gets up, looks over at my wrist, and says he's going to bed. I didn't have the heart to tell him that Douglas Adams in *The Hitchhiker's Guide to the Galaxy* had already figured out "the meaning of life." He says, it's the number "42," which makes about as much sense as anything else.

11.

The next morning, I see Dr. Canter again, and this time in a small white interrogation-like room next to the nurse's station. She asks me a bunch of questions and has me fill out questionnaires about habits and my state of mind; I assume the clinical atmosphere of this room is more conducive to interrogation. Some of the questions are: *Is the world a bad place? Y or N? Do you think about hurting yourself or others? Y or N? Do you see or hear things that others don't? Y or N? etc., etc., etc.* I answer "yes" to almost everything except about hearing or seeing things that others don't, which isn't exactly accurate. Then she has me take an IQ test.

"You hear the voice of your dead friend, don't you?" she asks. It is as if she has tricked me, as the fluorescent lights flicker their approval overhead.

"Well, I guess so, but it's more like a conversation."

"Why do you think that is?"

"Because I don't have anyone else to talk to, or know anybody as smart as him."

Canter scribbles something in her notebook, then looks up. "Don't you think you could make some new friends?"

"Maybe, it's just that most people aren't that interesting."

"And he was?" she asks, narrowing her eyes.

"Yes, he could make anything interesting, especially uninteresting stuff."

"Like how?"

I think about it for a minute. "Like the job we had last summer at the lake working on a boat dock that hardly anybody ever came to. It was really tiresome, just standing around all day doing nothing. Once in a while we'd help people climb into and out of their canoes."

"So how did he make that more interesting?" she asked.

"Well, if someone was rude to us, an asshole or a guy just being obnoxious, Aaron would let go of the canoe just a little bit as they were getting into it and they'd wobble a bit, freak out, and sometimes just tip right over into the water and start screaming and flailing about."

"And this was funny to you?"

"Yeah. Of course, it was. Just cause you're doing some crappy job doesn't mean people can treat you like shit."

She raises her eyebrows and probably says a silent, Huh. She looks at me to continue.

"So, one time this *whole* mean family fell into the water and started flailing around and flapping their arms and yelling at us so loud that we got to laughing so hard that we started crying and couldn't even help them out of the water. We got fired, of course, but it was worth it. I would start tearing up and laugh for weeks after that just thinking about it."

"What did your parents think of you getting fired?"

"My parents were pissed when they heard from the manager why we were fired. But Aaron insisted that the guy did us a service. 'A job like that could kill a person's desire to live,' he said. No matter how boring anything was, he could somehow make it at least interesting."

She takes a deep breath. "So how do you feel about things now, I mean now that you're here? Do you feel like you need to take your life and your future a little more seriously, that maybe your friend Aaron wasn't serious enough?" She looks down at her paper file. "I mean, he did die driving recklessly."

Now I narrow my eyes at her. "Did I tell you the woman who found his dead body saw a light shooting out of it up into the sky?" I tried to calm down. "Wonder if that would happen to you, Doctor Canter?"

She takes a deep breath. "Sorry, didn't mean to taint your friend's memory." I nod my head. "So, what were your plans before he passed on?"

"We were going to go to Costa Rica and be river rafting guides and learn how to surf."

"And what about your plans now? Have you thought about going to college? Isn't that the plan that you and your parents came up with?"

"It was more like their plan, because I honestly don't know what to do."

"Well, from your high school transcript, you did well in some subjects. So, I think you'd enjoy college; you can take courses in what interests you." I nod my head. A good point. She now sits back for her final assessment. "Jackson, I think that you're smart enough to do whatever you put your mind to. Just think about it, okay? We'll talk more next time."

"Okay," I say and nod my head, as she gathers all her papers for my file and stands up.

"Things are going to be okay for you," she says, smiling widely. I want to believe her, but I think that it's a bad sign that she needs an accordion folder to hold all the papers about what is wrong with me.

"How is it for you here in the hospital?" she asks, as we are walking out of the interrogation room.

"It's all right. They feed me well and I like the company. Some of the patients are interesting."

She actually smirks. "To say the least," and then catches herself. "How do you feel on the medication?"

"A little bit like my head got electrocuted. Is that good?"

"I don't know. Do you mean energized?"

"I guess. It's like my brain is being jump-started, like I said."

"Well, I think that may be a good thing, Jackson. Don't you?" she asks.

I then hear Aaron say, "*Tell her that you want off that shit asap, buddy. There's not a damn thing wrong with you. This capitalist dog-eat-dog world is the fucking problem. They're trying to turn you into some kind dull, dumb robot who'll take orders and*

be a good factory worker! We've got bigger plans than that for you!
You tell her that!"

I don't say anything. She seems so kind and well-intentioned that maybe she has a point.

"Whatever you say, Doctor." She nods her head, seems to like that.

I go back to my room, lay in bed and look out the window. The sun is shining faintly through the silt-stained window. The room's not bad. I've stayed in motel rooms that were a lot worse, especially on this last road trip to hell. Most of all I like the fact that I can't see myself in the cloudy reflection of the plastic mirror in the bathroom. I'm kind of tired of being my old self right now, honestly.

My roommate rolls over and yells, "Time? Time? What's the Time?!

I tell him, "3 o'clock."

"AM or PM?!" He yells again.

I decide to alter our routine a bit. "Greenwich Standard Time," I tell him

He pauses, as if he were calculating the time zone difference. "Okay. Thanks roommate," he says, rolls over and goes back to sleep, and I return to staring out the window.

12.

It's break time in the group room where I sit writing with my yellow legal pad. Everyone's ambling around, watching TV, or talking to themselves. I mind my own business. A girl named Amy just left the hospital. Her fiancé came to take her away. She was here because of a stress-induced stroke of some kind. Amy was about six feet tall and had a kind of rounded look about her that's hard to describe. She wore giant round, red glasses and bright red lipstick and had a slightly dazed look in her eyes. When I first arrived in the Intensive Treatment Unit, she came out of her room and began talking to me like we were at a party.

"Hi, my name's Amy," she said, twirling her messy hair and giving me the eye. "What's your name?"

"Jackson," I said, looking around the room to make sure we were still on the psych ward, and it wasn't party time.

"So, Jackson. What brought you in?" she asked, as though asking me what I did for a living.

"A sort of suicide attempt," I said, glancing down at my nonexistent watch as though I had to be somewhere else soon.

"Oh, you poor thing," she said and looked down at my bandaged wrist near my nonexistent watch. "You poor, poor baby." She put her hand on my back and rubbed it gently. It was kind of calming really, and it was nice to be touched by someone so caringly, even if it was by a crazy-looking girl in the psych ward. At least I wasn't paying her.

"Well, we're going to nurse you back to health, Jackson. You can count on it." She had actually been a nurse I learned later.

The following week Amy would have me tell her about what had been going on in my life that led me here, and what I was worried about and what my hopes and dreams were for myself. She would talk to me in soothing tones, or comfort me by taking my hand in hers or stroking my back. She was a pretty understanding person. She seemed genuinely concerned with who I was, a little too concerned sometimes, honestly, but sweet and kind.

Amy was especially kind to the old Polish man who won't eat; she told me she used to work in a nursing home in Florida. She'd feed the old Polish man milk and help him walk around, when it would be kinder to just let him die. Television and milk, that's all the old Polish man wants. He sleeps, watches television, drinks his milk, and he pees and shits himself wherever he is.

"I piss, I piss!" He always says afterwards. "I shit, I shit!" I think he'd rather be dead than living like this, or I would at least. He's just too out of it to know any better now.

Like I said, Amy would hold my hand sometimes, the one with the cut on the wrist. She would even pray for me. Sometimes she would make me repeat the prayer. I didn't mind. The recitation would nearly put me to sleep along with the medication. It's crazy to me that someone that I just met in the psych ward could be more understanding and compassionate than the people back home like my girlfriend who I'd known for a long time.

As she left, Amy gave me her address and phone number and handed me a note that said: "What can I say? I feel your Pain and Anguish. I don't know what could have provoked that kind of sadness. I'm truly sorry."

After Amy leaves, I go back to my room and stand for hours looking through my reflection out the window, trying to make sense of all of this mania, mine and others. I watch as kids yell and play tag in the street below on their way home from school, and I think how I used to be like them, a carefree kid without a worry in the world. Now I feel like a defective product that has been sent back to the plant to be repaired or discarded. I don't function properly. I look up at the sky and think to myself, "Somebody up there botched their job."

I'm called away to see my therapist again in the tiny white-walled room that seems to be shrinking around me. In the meeting that feels unending, Dr. Canter tells me that my friend's deaths, the breakup with Caitlin, and all the acid I was taking, the weed I was smoking, and the drinking I was doing to cope with my depression caused a kind of *break* in my mind. And as a result of that, she says that I developed severe major depression but that I'm probably not schizophrenic, so I've got that going for me. Crazy but not *seriously* crazy. That thought made me smile.

"I think this is probably just a normal reaction to the shit proposition that life really is," I tell her.

"Jackson, you're just seeing things through a foggy lens. We're working on clearing that lens."

She says that along with the medication, I'll need to stop isolating myself and engage in something she calls Cognitive Behavioral Therapy. This basically means that I'll have to expose myself to environments that I am fearful of—the outside world and being around people. This basically means that I'll need to get a job, pay bills, go to church, build a career. In other words, join the rat race and do all that other crap. *Life* really.

I now hear Aaron, "*Buddy, what do you think about jumping out of a helicopter in Alaska and skiing down Mt. Denali, fighting a Grizzly Bear at the bottom of the run, and then getting blitzed at the bar? This honestly sounds like a better proposition than all this other horseshit . . . . Whaddya think?*"

Yeah, I think you're right, bro.

"But with continued medication and therapy," Dr. Canter adds, "You can climb out of the rut." In other words, my mind is stuck in a major rut of Depression like a wagon wheel spinning uselessly on a waterlogged and overused trail digging itself deeper and deeper into the mud, as I'm about to be snowed in like the

Donner Party in a mountain pass. And we all know what happened to them.

I think about all of this psyche analysis looking out at the peaceful neighborhood below with the leaves blowing around slowly on the ground, a blue sky up above, framed by the window and separated. I'm here in my pajamas, slippers, at nineteen with my wrist slit and wrapped with bandages, tagged with my medical ID – SICK.

"Well," Canter says in a merry tone, "I think that does it for today." She stands up, but I remain sitting. "Is there anything else you need to say, Jackson?" she asks me.

"Yeah, Doctor. Could you give me a back rub like Amy used to?"

Dr. Canter looks shocked at this suggestion. "I'm sorry, but we can't touch the patients."

I felt like saying, mimicking Yoda from *Star Wars*, "And that is why you fail."

13.

Another day.

An older woman named Jane keeps ringing her bell for help, and it snaps me out of my thought track as I sit in the group room staring out the windows and thinking of what I'm going to do with my life.

Finally, I've heard enough. "What do you need, Jane?" I ask her so she'll stop ringing her goddamn bell.

"I need to make a phone call," she says all angrily like it's my problem or something. "*And* I need my roommate to give my social worker my glasses so that she can bring them to me. That's what I need! That stupid cow can't do anything right! I told her that I can't see a damn thing without them glasses."

"Okay, Jane," I say. "Give me a minute." I stand up and go to my room to get thirty-five cents for her to make the goddamn call. My roommate is asleep, and I try not to wake him as I shuffle through my small wooden chest of drawers looking for change. I finally find the coins and take them back to Jane so that she'll stop ringing her bell.

"Thank you, dear boy," she says. She smiles at me, as if she's going to say, "I've always depended on the kindness of strangers." It's a line I read from a stupid play in English class - I'm not a big fan of plays. She now wobbles across the room and climbs into one of the phone booths along the wall, and I go back to staring out the window.

This afternoon was one of our few group meetings that my overweight and sad roommate made. I told the group that I was glad that he was my roomy, since we're supposed to say something nice about someone else. He smiled shyly like a little kid—all of us are like little kids desperate for the attention and approval of others. Then, he said, "I saw Jackson the day he came. He was looking into my room and I thought to myself, I hope he's my roommate. He looks like a nice guy. He looks like he'll keep his things clean and keep to himself. I'm glad that he's my roommate too."

I began to feel bad for him as I tried to picture his life on the outside. He doesn't seem to have a damn thing to hold onto in this world. No one calls for him. No one comes by. No one seems to give a shit about him. And he's a mess and too broken to do anything about it. He's fallen apart and has no clue how to put himself back together again. And therapy doesn't seem to be helping him much. He's just one of the people who slipped through the cracks in life. He seeks comfort in his sleep. Sleep is his escape. I guess, like drinking was mine. Sleep is his drug, better than anything the doctors could give him, except a loaded gun, and even then, I don't think that he'd have the energy to use it.

Later on, that night, we have oatmeal cookies, skim milk, and apple juice for our late- night snack. We all gather around the table like a pack of hungry kids. Koran stands next to the table making sure that everybody gets something.

"You need two cookies, Jackson," she says, putting them on my plate. "You're lookin' kinda thin. You need to put some weight on them bones."

"Thanks Koran," I say smiling.

Steven and I sit down at one of the tables together.

"It's 9:30. I'm usually in bed by now," he says. "But I wanted to stay up and talk to you." I look back expectantly, wondering if he's finally going to share "the meaning of life." Instead, he tells me, "I'm moving to the Y soon. I could find a room there for you too, ya know. We could be neighbors."

"Yeah, that would be pretty cool, Steven."

"Yeah, it would," he says. "We could calm our minds together . . . You know, I've been admitted to the hospital eighteen times. I'm on five different medications." He looks at me seriously. "I have an approach to suffering that could help you."

"Oh yeah? What?" I ask, feeling hopeful. Really. I could use some help about now.

"There's joy in suffering."

This is deep. I take a moment to feel my way through it. "You think?"

"Yeah, suffering is a sanctification process. Suffering makes you, um . . . makes you, um . . . whole," he says. I nod my head. Steven stands up and wanders back to his room.

I move to the sofa and stare out the windows and think about this. After a while, Koran comes over and sits next to me. We stare out the window together. Finally, she says, "What you thinkin' about Jackson?"

"Suffering."

"Why you thinkin' about that Jackson?" she says, and starts laughing and I start laughing too. "You crazy! You miss Amy, don't you?"

"I miss her rubbing my back," I say, smiling.

"You crazy. I'll rub on your back, Jackson."

I look at her earnestly, "Koran, how did you end up in here?"

She turns her head to me, looking at me like I'm crazy. "Jackson… You really wanna hear all that bullshit?"

"Yeah. I want to know your story, why you're here. Because you're amazing to me, Koran."

She smiles at me, puts her hand on my back. "You just plain crazy Jackson. So, how much of my story are we talkin'?"

"All of it."

"All a my story…?" She looks me dead in the eyes, then turns and looks out the window and takes a deep breath as she rests her hands in her lap. "Ok Jackson." She starts, "You sure you wanna hear it?" I nod my head. "My momma was a crackhead…And my daddy, he wasn't never around. I got six brothers and sisters. We all lived in a one-bedroom apartment with roaches, in the projects. We didn't have no television 'cause my momma pawned it off to buy drugs. And we didn't have no food, cause my momma spent all the welfare money on drugs. So, me and my brothers and sisters, we practically lived on the streets, beggin' people for money to buy food wit'." Koran stops for a second, takes another deep breath, lets it out as her eyes start to water. "Then she started trickin' to make money to support her habit. After that, there was always strange men around…" She shakes her head. Her face looks drained as she stares out the windows into the darkness, as though trying to shake off the past. "You sure you wanna hear all this shit, Jackson?"

"Yeah."

She nods her head solemnly. "After that it was all a damn mess. By the time I was seventeen I was strung out on drugs, livin' in a motel with a man who beat on me. It got worse and I had to run. I lived on the streets. Until, somehow or another, I made it to a shelter, and they got me into a rehab facility and then a home for battered women and helped me get on my feet and get a job. I went to them sorry ass AA meetings and all that. But I couldn't never stay clean for long." She looks back at me, smirks, and shrugs her shoulders. "It would always just start off with a sip of vodka when I was feeling down or scared or started thinkin' too much about things. And then once I got a taste, I'd start drinkin' more. I could play it off for a while, but then I'd start usin' again, and it wouldn't take long before I'd lose my job, then get kicked out of the women's home. I'd end up on the street again with some triflin'-ass man who'd take me in and say all the right things, then just end up beatin' on me like all the rest of them. And I'd run. I've been runnin' in and out of shelters and rehabs and halfway houses ever since. And now, since I started thinkin' about takin' my own life, they've been puttin' me in these damn psych wards."

There's a long silence that follows as we both stare out the windows. "My momma got sober and found Jesus, and she's been helpin' me out some." She shakes her head. "Jackson. You're a good person. And you look good and you talk good, and you got all your teeth and you got a family that loves you. I don't know why you're in this stinkin' place with all these crazy-ass people."

I laugh and look back at her, all the pain and suffering of her life clearly etched into her lined face, and I put my face in my hands and break down sobbing. It is as if a dam has broken, and I cry not just for Koran and her sad life but all the people here, myself included. The crying is uncontrollable now. She puts her hand on my back and rubs it. A nurse comes over and asks if I'm all right.

"It's all just catchin' up with him. Leave him be," Koran says.

The nurse shakes her head and walks away. I sit up. Some of the other patients are looking at me, nodding their heads, smiling. People with *really* hard lives. And me? I'm falling apart because I lost a friend and think life is shitty. Big fucking deal.

I look at Koran. "Koran. I think you're amazing."

She smiles. "Just cause I said I'd give you a back rub, don't go askin' for sex from me now, Jackson."

I look back at her startled, and then I start laughing so hard it brings tears to my eyes again. And soon everybody in the break room is laughing along with me, not even knowing what they're laughing about.

14.

I wake at 7:45. It's foggy out again. I get dressed, start making up my bed. My roommate rolls over and screams, "Time! Time! What time is it?!" I look at the clock and tell him, and he yells, "AM or PM?!" Time doesn't matter to him anymore. He's in his own private hell, shut off from this one. But then, aren't we all.

"AM," I say.

"Oh, that's good," he says, rolls over and goes back to sleep.

At breakfast Steven comes over and sits down next to me. "I think your book ought to be a journal like Anne Frank's."

I read her book in English class and liked it a lot. "I don't think people will believe that demons are after me," I tell him.

He looks at me out the side of his glasses. "I believe you, Jackson. You've got *Hospital Eyes*. And there's only three ways you can get Hospital Eyes—being chased by demons, doing too many drugs (which just opens yourself up to demons), and being hospitalized long-term. You haven't been in the hospital long enough yet to get that look. So, it has to be that seen demons." I thought it was kind of him to skip the drug qualification.

"What do you think they want, Steven?"

He looks sideways at me as though I should know better. "Your soul, of course. And to feed on your pain until they do. You need God, Jackson . . . Only He can help you." Steven now reaches into his pocket and hands me a worn-out, folded-up piece of paper. It's the number to the YMCA. "Give them a call about a room, Jackson." Then his Hospital Eyes seem to drift off.

"Are you really writing a book?" he asks curiously, as he begins rocking back and forth, rubbing his head. He hasn't touched his breakfast. I ask him if he's okay. He says he didn't sleep well, that he's worried about getting out and finding a job. He stands up and goes back to his room to lie down. I pick up his tray and bus it for him.

There are three showers on the ward. I haven't showered since I've got here because they're so nasty, but now I'm stinky, no doubt about it. So, after breakfast I go to inspect the showers. The first one seems the cleanest, so I take it. I alert the nurses station of my showering. The water pressure is low, and the water is very cold for the first fifteen minutes, but the shower is relatively clean and has a floor mat. That's what's important to me now—clean walls and floor mats. One of the male nurses stands outside the shower and calls my name once in a while to make sure that I'm not trying to hurt myself. This monitoring bothers me the most, makes me realize how sick I am of all this oversight. Since I can't tell the doctors what I really feel about it, I decide that I need to write it all out.

Afterward, I head back to my room, pull out my legal pad and pen, and go to the rec room. Steven has inspired me. I start to think about my book seriously. I like the journal idea. It allows you to scattershot your impressions and not have to create a regular storyline. Don't think my mind is clear enough for that, not right now. I start to jot down some of my earliest childhood memories.

1: I remember riding my BMX bike with my friends to the little corner store, a couple miles from my house, to buy baseball cards. I had a silver and black Diamond Back BMX with a black-and-white checkerboard handlebar pad. Tyler had a black Redline and Josh an electric-blue GT. Riding through the streets in the sunshine on the weekend with the smell of freshly cut grass in the air was the closest thing to freedom an eight year old Mormon boy could hope for. I felt so grown up. We'd get to the store, park our bikes out front, and run inside to pick out the Topps baseball card packs. We hoped to snag cards of Jose Canseco, Mark McGwire, or Dwight Gooden.

We'd throw our change on the counter and run out to open up our packs. Most of the time we'd get no-name baseball players, but once in a while, one of us would get lucky with a card that was worth something. Each pack of cards came with a pink stick of bubble gum that was as brittle as a piece of shale and covered in a strange thin white chalky film. It wasn't that good and didn't last that long, but we'd shove it all in our mouths as part of the ritual

and then ride our bikes home like we were kings of the world.

What I ask myself, without writing it down, is how such a normal childhood could end up here, me with a slashed wrist in a psych ward in San Francisco? Now, I skip a space on my journal page and write this question down. If I'm going to figure out how to get out of here, I've got to trace my steps up to that night in the motel room guzzling champagne and cutting myself. My roommate farts. A definite sign.

Later that morning, it's time for a smoke break out on the concrete terrace in the warm sunshine. Ahmad's mumbling to himself, his hair scattered wild off his head, and Jane is laughing to herself, her hair all greasy and matted. My therapist handed me a couple packs of cigarettes at our last session as I had asked for previously. I don't really smoke that much, so I give most of them away to the other patients. It's nice to be outside and feel the fresh air before the smoke haze dampens it. It feels less threatening out here than when I first arrived. But with each drag off my cigarette, my brain seems to *sizzle,* as though I can feel every neuron nervously lighting up. It must be the medication combination. I continue to think about my situation, not as negatively now after hearing Koran's story and starting my journal, as the white glare from the sun sears my eyes. I watch detached, as my hands tremble a bit, the cigarette dangling loosely between my forefingers as anxiety floods my system. I put my smoke out in one of the potted plants and go back inside seeking shelter.

Shelly, the skinny girl with scraggly hair and clothes, is laughing at the television in the group room, talking to it. She is always laughing and talking to the television. No one ever pays her much mind. I can't exactly understand what she's saying, but it seems important to her. She points her finger and swears at the television, scolding it like she's having a conversation with the people on TV.

Koran stands in the doorway of the smoke terrace. "Shelly hears *them* voices," she says to me, as she takes a drag off of her cigarette.

"Who doesn't?" I say, but not too convincingly. Koran catches my tone and smiles. "Steven says that demons are feeding on my soul."

"You got a good soul Jackson. You best start takin' care of it ." She says, matter of factly.

Jane saves me a seat at lunch as she does every day now because I get things for her when she rings that damn annoying bell. One of the nurses brought her out in a wheelchair. She's not supposed to stand up much because she has a hard time walking, and the nurses are worried that she will fall and hurt herself. So, they gave her a little bell to ring when she needs something. The nurses are supposed to get her what she needs, but they're usually too busy, and I don't have anything else to do, so I help her. Besides, as I've said, I can't stand her ringing her goddamned bell all the time. As we eat, she says to me, "You know I wish something would happen."

"Like what, Jane?"

"Well, that you would come visit me when you get out."

I tell her that I'll try. At least she won't be able to summon me with a bell ring.

"Recreation," the intercom crackles, and I put my food tray away in one of the metal carts that they roll in and out of the ward before and after meals. I go back to my room to continue writing which is *my* recreation. I find it relaxing.

Greg, the Greek guy with a dark stubble beard, starts singing loudly, and it resonates up and down the hall of the ward. At lunch Koran told him that he had a good voice. He smiled like an embarrassed little kid. Now he's walking up and down the hall and singing. "I'm gonna get out my John Travolta outfits and go dancing!" he yells. The big head nurse tells him to shut up because one of the doctors is on the phone. But he doesn't stop. He starts singing again at the top of his lungs off key, *You're a Hard Habit to Break!* This song is fairly appropriate for our psyche ward.

That afternoon, two cute College interns come into my room to see if they can ask me some questions. I try to act as natural as possible. I'm ashamed to be seen as a mental patient subject and realize that I'll probably never have a girlfriend again, or nobody as pretty as these two. The interns sit down in a couple of the beat-up chairs in my room. Their skirts are short, and I occasionally glance at their legs.

"So, first question. What exactly brought you here?" Jennifer, the prettier of the two, asks.

"A suicide attempt." I look down at my wrist and the hospital bracelet that tags me as *sick*. I can feel my cheeks flushing. The girls look uncomfortable.

"Next question. How would you rate the quality of your home life?" Brittany, the other girl, asks. She's pretty in a tomboy way.

"On a scale of 1-10, or on a sliding scale?" They look at each other unsure. "I'm just joking. My home life was fine. My parents loved me and all that. They didn't really understand what was going on with me recently, and neither did I. But since coming here, I really appreciate how much they cared for me growing up. So, I'd give them almost an 8 on a scale of 10. They would have had a 9 if they'd let me stay up later." They smile at this and I feel like I haven't yet lost my touch.

"What do you feel are the biggest stressors that led to you being here?"

"Well, my best friend died, and after that I felt kind of lost and sad, I guess." At this, they both say, "Aww . . . " Like someone just pulled out a puppy and started grooming it. Jennifer, with the pert brown hair looks like she should be in a shampoo commercial, puts down the questionnaire, leans forward and asks, "What happened?"

"Yeah, what happened, Jackson?" Brittany, with the blond ponytail and dazzling smile who also looks like she should be in a commercial, singing about how good life is, follows up. And I'm so stunned by both of them staring at me and not being freaked out by my condition that I just start rambling and spilling out my guts. For the first time since I've come here, I'm not feeling so sad and embarassed about it all. As I talk, it's almost like I can see myself from far away, with my arms and hands moving animatedly and the two girls just sitting there, looking at me like they *understand.* And tears come to our eyes.

Finally, Jennifer, who appears to be the leader, closes her notebook and looks earnestly back at me. "Thank you, Jackson, for being so honest with us. We both think you're on the road to recovery. You're going to be *okay.*"

I nod my head. It's good to hear this assessment from a third party, or at least someone besides the white coats. Suddenly, my roommate rolls over in his sleep and says, "Do you want to have sex?" He then rolls back over and starts snoring. This startles all three of us. Then Jennifer starts to laugh. As they leave the room, Jennifer looks over her shoulder at me, as if to say, look me up when you get out.

This puts a big, stupid smile on my face for the whole day. The others notice it but don't say anything. However, some of the male patients start pestering the girls for interviews as they make their rounds.

15.

Greg, the Greek, has slicked back his hair this morning. He has a dark crazy look in his eyes. I tell him that he looks like the devil. He just turns and smiles wickedly, and I swear I can smell Sulphur.

I tell Steven about it at breakfast.

"Sulfur's the smell of the Devil, Jackson."

"It could have been from one of the toilets. They put chemicals in them."

He smirks, "Yeah well, with the drugs they give us and food we're fed here I'm sure our shit is pretty toxic."

I laugh. "You got a point, Steven."

"But, no, it's the devil. This is where he wants you Jackson, locked away and unable to share your smile with the world."

Steven is leaving this morning. He has his suitcase packed and ready sitting on the floor next to him at breakfast. He's nervous and doesn't touch his food again. Guess he doesn't want to take that Sulphur smell back with him.

"I'm disappointed I couldn't convert you Jackson. You need God."

I try to ease his separation anxiety. "I know, Steven. I'm trying." This makes him smile; his stay here hasn't been a waste after all.

One of the nurses comes in and calls out Steven's name. "It's time for you to go now. The world awaits you, Steven." This doesn't seem to cheer him up.

"Bye Jackson," he says, looking blankly ahead as he picks up his suitcase, stands up and shuffles out. He looks disheveled, and there are clothes hanging out of his suitcase.

I smell Sulphur again and look up to see Greg pacing in the corner, watching us. I feel like he's the devil today, trying to take away Steven's light.

An hour or so later, Steven is knocking on the door of the Unit, trying to come back. "Can you please let me back in guys," he pleads. Greg paces up and down the halls pulling his hair, laughing wildly, with a sinister look in his eyes. It's heartbreaking to watch Steven. I yell at Greg, "Shut the hell up!" He laughs louder. Steven looks so pitiful, standing outside the door peering through the small window onto our ward. I go over and talk to him through the door, trying to comfort him some.

"I can't take it out there, Jackson. I'm no good at living." Steven cackles at the other end of the hallway.

"It'll be okay, Steven. You'll meet a lot of nice people at the Y, and I'll call you when I get out."

"Promise?"

"Yeah, I promise."

"Call my mother's number first. I might stay there to get her situated."

The head nurse comes over and tells him he needs to go home. A minute later security guards arrive and take him away as Greg laughs maniacly.

I don't really feel like going to any of the groups or eating lunch, and I just lay in my room the rest of the day. Steven's desperation and Greg's reaction scares me.

Finally, one of the nurses, Judy, makes me come out for dinner. I sit quietly alone at the table unable to eat any of the food, and then go back to my room to lie down and think. The same nurse sticks her head in the door to see if I'm okay.

I want to ease her concern, so I repeat a line I saw in an old Cary Grant movie that was playing in the background at one of the motels I stayed at, "Judy, Judy, Judy."

She smiles. "That's better, Jackson."

Later on in the evening, as I head out for evening snacks, Koran's mother comes walking over towards me, slowly, with her big pink wool coat, her pink hat and her worn steel-rimmed glasses. You see this look in old black women in the movies or on television. She says, "God bless you, son."

I don't know what I did, but she smiles at me, hugs me and my heart swells.

"Koran says you's a good friend to her son. I preciate that."

"She's very sweet to me."

"Koran says that she told you all bout her struggles and that you didn't judge her for nothin'. You a good person, Jackson."

"Thank you, Miss Williams."

"God bless you, son."

Just seeing how proudly Miss Williams held herself up and how kind she was, while knowing all that she'd been through, it gave me hope for Koran's recovery.

After all the visitors are gone, the nurses bring us out a couple of trays of stuff for our late-night snack: cookies, milk, apple juice, bananas and graham crackers. I'm hungry now and eat a couple of cookies and a banana and drink a carton of milk. Afterward, I go to my room to sit and write. My roommate spins over on his side, "Time! Time! What time is it?!" But before I can tell him, he falls back to sleep.

Not long after I've fallen asleep myself, Koran comes to our open door.

"Jackson, Jackson, come on outta your room now. Put on your slacks and come on out here," she says.

She seems stressed out. Maybe it was her mother's visit.

"Okay," I say. "Give me a minute."

Koran waits down the hall for me. The medication makes her feet move fast tonight. She can't hold still and doesn't seem to be thinking clearly. She leads me out into the group room, and we sit down on one of the sofas but don't talk. Maybe she had a bad dream and just wants company. After a while, she tells me to stay, shuffles around the ward for a minute, distracted, then walks down the hall to her room and doesn't return. I think she just wants to know that I'm around, that someone is here who cares about her. And I go back to bed.

The next day Dr. Canter sits across from me, nestled behind her desk in her comfortable, cozy—but not too cozy—office with an air of genuine concern and professionalism.

"So, I hear you've been interacting with the other patients and making some friends?"

"Yeah, I guess. There's not much to do here, and they're the only ones to talk to, so you know. I make do."

"Does it feel good to make some connections, Jackson?"

"It makes me kind of sad really," I say and look out the window at the fog rolling in over the buildings. "I mean, these people have *real* problems."

"Yes, most of the patients here are pretty bad off. But you, on the other hand, still have your youth, your health, and your mind. How are you feeling in general?"

"Okay, I guess, my life doesn't seem so bad by comparison. In fact, after hearing Koran's story, I feel like a fraud for being here."

"Yes, she's had a rough go of it, but she tells me you're her best friend ever."

That puts a smile on my face.

"And, speaking of friends, how is Aaron?"

"I don't know. Still dead, I think." She smiles at this quip. "I haven't really been talking to him lately."

"That could be because you're making some real human connections again. You're getting better, Jackson."

I don't know what to say to that, so I just smile. The session is over, and I head back to my room.

My room smells like a dirty laundry basket. I think my roommate needs a shower. He rolls over and groans as if reading my mind. I lay down on my bed and look for planes outside my window. I think about what my therapist said about Aaron. And I don't know if he's an angel guiding me from the other side, or maybe just a security blanket that I'll just forget one day and realize that I don't need anymore.

16.

It's music and smoke-break time. I head out to the group room. Greg just woke up Bill, his new roommate, the big guy who looks like a bricklayer or something, to ask him for a cigarette. Now Bill is wandering around the ward half-asleep, trying to open the doors to get out. He's all confused, talking to the nurses and everyone else, mumbling to himself and completely out of it. He's banging on the doors and yelling, "LET ME THE FUCK OUTTA HERE! I'M GONNA BE LATE FOR WORK, YOU ASSHOLES!" He storms over to the nurse's station in a semi-trance asking how to get out of the ward. Then he wakes up all of a sudden and figures out where he is, as the nurses tell him that he can't leave. He yells, "WHO THE FUCK WOKE ME UP?! WHO THE FUCK WOKE ME UP?!" His hair is wet from sweat and his fists are clenched tightly. He's dazed and angry.

Greg is hiding by the radio in the group room across from the nurses' station. No one answers. The male nurses are called to the ward. Bill looks like he could easily kill everyone with his bare hands. He's awake now and grabs one of his cigs from the nurse's station. He then wanders into the eating/smoking/television/radio room. He listens to the music being played for a minute, then asks stridently to no one in particular, "How 'bout if I DJ the radio and change the fuckin' station?" That's usually Greg's job during music time, but he stands up quickly and moves away from it. Everyone watches as Bill strides boldly across the sunlit linoleum floor, sits down and scans the dial of the radio, then turns up a classic rock song announcing to the room, smiling, "This is a great fucking song!" It's *Satisfaction* by the Rolling Stones. Bill sings along with lyrics, "Can't get no satisfaction . . ." A few of the others tap their fingers to the beat. This may be the ward's theme song.

Jane leans over to me, "I can't get pregnant," she says.

"That's great," I tell her, "I can't either." She nods her head.

After the song ends Greg wanders around the ward singing loudly, off-key, "You're a hard habit to breakkkkk!"

At Group that afternoon, Bill starts telling us his story. Life has never let up on him. He's tried but life keeps dictating the terms. He looks and sounds like an insane Paul Bunyan. He's an Army vet and wears a tool belt to work, carries a lunch box, and dons a hard hat. Suddenly, Bill looks over at me and says, "You 'tink you got problems? Try going through life big, dumb, and German!" He holds his badly distorted trigger finger up that he got from firing his M16 endlessly in Vietnam, and laughs hysterically, smiling crazily at me. He's been through hell—too much cocaine, too much work, and too much life. His distorted finger and his fried mind are his testaments to it. Apparently, Bill wrote a death threat to his boss because he was passed over for a promotion. He no doubt figured that somewhere along the line in life he'd more than earned it. When confronted with the disapointment, he finally snapped, and it took four security guards to corral him until the cops came.

"I told that sonofabitch, no-good, piece-of-shit boss that I was gonna kill him, real good! Rip his fuckin head off and shit down his scrawny little neck. He started trembling like a little girl, and that alone was worth the trouble," he says. Bill gets that look in his eyes when he smiles at you like he's killed people, like he wouldn't flinch to wring your neck. Bill now looks over and smiles at me. I flinch.

After group it's lunch time. Man, do I need a break from Bill.

At meal times however, it's often difficult to eat with everyone sitting around like zombies, slobbering, mumbling to themselves and coughing on your food. Their sickness invading my mind like a viral plague. I try to keep my head down and not look at anyone. The longer that I'm here, the more able I am to tune it all out and just eat. I sit by Jane for most of the meals because she always saves me a seat. I'd rather sit by Koran, but she tells me to be nice to Jane and sit by her.

"You be nice to that crazy old lady now. You hear me?" Koran scolds me. "She likes you."

"Yeah," I tell her, "she likes me too much, Koran. She told me she can't get pregnant. Like, she's open for business." Koran looks at me crazily then laughs her infectious laugh at this.

"Oh, you crazy Jackson!" she says. "Sit down now by that old woman now and make her feel good." So, I do.

"I want to go out on a date," Jane says when I sit down next to her. She's fifty-two and a mess. There's a big swing in her step due to a bad hip, even when the nurses hold her good arm to walk. Her teeth are rotted, broken and yellowed. Her hair's all greasy, and she holds her hands in a strange position, with one deformed arm that's always held at an angle close to her chest like a kangaroo. This all makes her look rather helpless. But she is helpless. This is the only place she can survive.

After lunch I tell Koran that I don't want to go out on a date with Jane when I get out of here. She laughs wildly.

"Jackson, that woman, she likes you. Now you be nice to her while you here, and you get things for her like you been doin'. And you don't have to go out on no date with her, 'cause she'll never get out of here. Just you be nice to her while you're here! Okay?"

"Okay, Koran. You're the boss." She likes that.

I smile at her.

"You crazy, Jackson," she says.

I don't know why but I find myself thinking back to my first sexual experience at my aunt & uncle's house in Reno, when I was 11 or something. My cousin, Leslie, was 13. She wore all black, had Doc Martin boots and band pins, like *The Cure, The Smiths*, and *The Thompson Twins* on the torn-up Levi jacket she always wore. Her blonde hair was always ratted up, and she had a nose piercing. I thought she was the coolest person in the world. Every year we'd drive to Reno from Salt Lake City to stay with my Mom's sister who was the black sheep of the family, what the Mormon's called a *Jack Mormon*—someone who was no longer a practicing Mormon.

My parents, my aunt and uncle all went out on the town for a night of gambling, and drinking for the Jack Mormons, and left me and my cousin home alone. A handful of her neighborhood friends came over, boys and girls. They were drinking beer and smoking weed. They pulled out a bunch of sleeping bags, took them in the backyard, and we all played *truth or dare* under the stars. I remember it was still warm out and everyone was just daring each other to take off their clothes. One of the girls dared me to take off my T-shirt.

"Jackson doesn't have to if he doesn't want to!" Leslie told her.

"Then he has to drink!" an older boy, the ring-leader, said and handed me a beer.

"No!" she said. But I didn't want everyone to think I was a lame and dutiful Mormon from Utah, so I grabbed a beer and took a long swig. My cousin and all her friends started laughing. I had my swimsuit on from earlier, so I just took my T-shirt off, and they all clapped and started to disrobe. By the time everyone else got down to their underwear, they were all a little drunk and started jumping in the pool. Leslie had actual boobs, and you could see them right through her bra in the pool. I couldn't stop staring at them. She caught me looking, and I blushed as she yelled, "Jackson!"

"Let's play something!" the ring-leader yelled, and everyone piled out of the pool and onto blankets and sleeping bags that were spread out over the yard. It was almost cool out now, and people began covering themselves up with the blankets and climbing into the sleeping bags. Boys and girls started naturally pairing off.

"Come get under my blanket, Jackson," Leslie called to me. When I slipped under it, she pressed her boobs up against me and put her arm around me. She was warm and comforting, and I felt bad about being attracted to her.

"Okay, everyone!" the ring-leader yelled. "Everyone has to take a swig of beer and a hit of weed because we're playing sleeping-bag roulette! Whoever you're next to, you have to get in a sleeping bag with them for the next 10 minutes!" He looked at us. "Even if they're your cousin!" I don't remember a lot of the details about what happened next, except that I drank some more beer and the sky began to sway as I climbed into a sleeping bag next to my cousin. Her body was warm, her breath smelled like beer. She took off her bra and told me to touch her while she reached into my bathing suit and rubbed my dick. I don't remember much else, but I don't think we did more than that. A couple years later, I heard that it got really bad for her.

17.

I'm sitting in the group room thinking about Leslie and what happened to her and how things can pile up, then quickly collapse, crushing you under the weight of it all. She started partying, drinking, smoking weed, then doing blow, then got hooked on pills.

She had to go to rehab the summer after her Junior year. During her senior year, I heard she started dating an older guy who drove an El Camino. Pretty soon after that she got pregnant and ended up dropping out of school. And just like that, her life was over. Last I heard she was living with her alcoholic mechanic boyfriend in a trailer park on the outskirts of Reno, fat as a blimp, still drinking and probably high on pills. I know I drank too much, smoked too much weed and sort of tried to kill myself, but that stopped my downward slide. I've got to get my head together before this all gets out of hand for me too.

I look over at Bill who is creating another ruckus. He's always giving the nurses shit, which is at least entertaining. He now tells everyone that he doesn't mind being here since he's on sick leave and getting paid.

"Sick leave!" he yells out in the group room. "That's what those son of a bitches are calling it! The only thing I'm sick of is that fuckin job! But they're paying me to be here! Can you believe that shit? This is a paid vacation!"

Everybody looks back wondering, I guess, how they can sign up and get them some "paid sick leave."

Bill loves the food here, and he usually eats two trays or the rest of someone else's, but never mine. He's got a problem with me. I can see that. He's always checking out what I'm doing, like I somehow threaten him, even if he could take my scrawny ass with one hand tied behind his back.

I now sit watching everyone in the group room as I take a personality test that one of the staff doctors gave me. Koran comes over to help me while Bill watches our exchange. She reads the next question: 'I see things or animals or people around me that others do not see. True or False?'

"False," Koran says. "Cus' if you tells em that you see or hear things, that means you must think you're a God, and then they'll crucify you, just like Jesus!" Then she points towards the people watching a talk show. "Watch out for TV now! You hear me?" I nod my head. "Cus that's what they be usin on the sick ones," she says, then wanders off around the ward. Bill's eyes were still glued to me from across the room.

Fifteen minutes later, Koran comes back again just as I'm about to finish the test, and adds, "Make sure you get a couple a them answers wrong, cus' if you's bein' *too* smart that gets you into trouble too. People don't like that neither and they'll crucify you for that, too!"

Bill watches me. I look back, put my hands in the air like I'm surrendering to the police and smile. I'm trying to convince him I'm not a problem he has to worry about. He shakes his head in disgust.

I hand in my test at the nurses' station. One of the nurses takes it to this new staff doctor in his makeshift office. I'm told to take a seat in the group room, and I'll be called. Twenty minutes later, the doctor—short, older, balding, bespectacled, and wearing a white lab coat—steps out and waves me over. The office is a tiny, white and windowless room with fluorescent lights that will fry your mind. He sits on a swivel-chair crammed in between two built-in desks along the wall next to cabinets bulging with files and medical books. My patient folder is spread out on the desk.

"Take a seat," he says, pointing to the swivel-chair opposite of him. We're almost touching knees. "All right, I've graded your test and read your file." He smiles reassuringly, or so it seems - he's got a look in his eyes that doesn't agree with me. "Well, you're definitely smart and not crazy, or at *least* not schizophrenic!"

"That's good news," I say.

"Not great," he replies, "because you're still *here*." He looks at me over his glasses with disapproval.

"So, I'm too smart to be in here, but too crazy to be out there?" I ask.

He laughs at this comment. "A real catch-22. Yep! That's one way to put it," he says. "But don't worry. We'll probably have you out of here in no time." *Probably*. That sounds somewhat encouraging, but then asks me a slew of stupid questions.

Afterward, I head out to the group room and tell Koran the doctor said I'm not crazy.

"I told you Jackson. You listen to me and you gonna be alright," she says. I don't bring up that she keeps telling me, 'You *crazy*, Jackson.'

Bill nods his head, no doubt hoping I'll be released soon and the threat to him minimized. He goes back to watching TV.

I head back to my room and stare out at the gray of the day, think about Caitlin and the slick wetness of her strawberry lipstick kisses. I'd give anything to kiss her again. I run my fingers through my greasy hair, and think about the people I know on the outside. I don't have anyone to call and even if I did, I wouldn't know what to say. They've all started to fade away, my friends from Salt Lake, like those dreams you have where people vaporize next to you, unexplainably. When I called home last night, my younger sister answered and said that my parents were out.

"You're lucky they're not here anyway Jackson," she said. "They don't know how to talk about all this stuff that's going on with you anyway. They just want things to go back to being normal."

"Me too."

"You know how they are, and how we don't ever talk about anything?"

"Yeah, I know." I sigh and look around at the dismal surroundings of the ward.

"They just want it all to go away and go back to pretending that life is perfect, that you're and that you're okay. Are you going to be okay?"

"Yeah, I'm going to be okay. I just got a little sad and confused, that's all."

"Ok. Just take care of yourself Jackson, and get yourself back together again. And don't try to change who you are to please them. I like you just the way you are, even if you are a little crazy," she says and laughs. It makes me smile. I tell her I love her and goodbye.

I look back out the window at the gray sky and start to flashback to everything that got me here. I feel myself getting hot, itchy, uncomfortable—no doubt triggered by the doctor's analysis. This is one of the few times I've really wanted to get out of here since I was admitted. I *have* to leave, I decide. I'm not crazy like these *other* people. And I don't want to be on this medication shit forever, just because I couldn't conform, because I couldn't accept this rattrap world of ours. I'm not crazy. *Life* is what's insane!

I paused expecting and then hearing Aaron in my head. *"That's right, buddy! You're not crazy. You just had a bad run. Life is what's insane. The whole world's falling apart; Americans have been turned into money-hungry drones who do nothing but work and consume crap. All the while, they're lying, cheating, stealing and desecrating the planet as they blindly try to keep up with the Joneses who are all happily hurling themselves into a fiery abyss! You're not crazy. You weren't made for this bullshit! We're going to start a 'Don't Give a Shit Revolution' and you're going to be the leader!"*

I think about what the doctor said, that I'm not schizophrenic, and that I'm too smart to be in here. But I'm still talking to my dead friend who's giving me life advice in a world I sometimes don't want to live in because it all seems so backwards and crazy. So, something's got to give. And if I'm not schizophrenic and I'm not *really* hearing Aaron's voice and he's not really an angel and I'm not *really* crazy, then maybe I just need to stop talking to Aaron? I mean, if he's not really talking to me, then it's got to be coming from my mind, and then, I'm okay. But thinking about it too much makes me feel *crazy*. Then I hear his voice again say, "You're gonna be okay, buddy."

18.

It's the first group of the day. This morning it's art therapy. Koran, Greg, Ahmad, Jane, Bill, and I are the only ones who make it to group. Most of us are either rubbing our eyes, yawning, or curling up in a chair with a blanket, like Koran.

Our therapist, Karen, who looks like she substitutes teaches at a nearby middle school, has brought in some art books to help inspire us for today's art session. But Bill's not having any of it.

"This is just stupid! How is any of this supposed to help us? Are we gonna become famous artists when we get outta here? Are *you* serious lady?" he asks the therapist who is looking slightly nervous. Most of the books are pretty lame, like the cover of one with its painting of a bowl of fruit on a wooden table.

"It's therapeutic to create something, and by creating something . . ." the therapist says before Bill cuts her off.

"Jesus! What a bunch of crap."

Karen squirms in her chair a little bit but continues, ". . . creating something can help us to process and release emotions."

I notice that there's a book with my first name on it— Jackson Pollock. The cover looks like a chaotic mess, like someone haphazardly spilled paint all over it. I pick it up. The painting somehow draws me in. The more I look at the chaotic and spattered painting, the more it mesmerizes me. I open up the book. There's page after page of wild, intense, and seemingly random, colorful paint-splatter images. But the more I stare at the paintings, the more I find an almost calming order beneath the chaos. When I was coloring as a kid, the teacher would always insist that you colored within the lines. Order and structure. But this guy doesn't obey the rules and goes off and finds his own meaning. I like that.

"You found a book you like?" Karen asks, happy to focus on someone besides Bill. I nod my head, still a little mesmerized. "That's good, Jackson. Here, take some paper and oil crayons," she says, placing a piece of construction paper and some oil crayons in front of me. I turn back and look at the inscription on the first inside page, a quote by Pollock, "Painting is self-discovery. Every good artist paints what he is."

I turn to the first painting again.

Koran sheds her blanket and steps over to see what's grabbed my attention. "That don't look like no painting I ever seen," Koran says. "It looks like that man just made a big ol' mess . . . Oh look," she says and points to the top of the page, "he's got the same name as you, Jackson!"

"I've got an idea!" I say, standing up and showing the group this painting. "Let's all just make a big ol' mess of paintings!"

Koran smiles at this. "You crazy, Jackson," she says. "But so be this Pollock guy . . . and us too, I guess."

Karen looks over at me and seems a little concerned by my idea, as she finishes handing out the materials. Greg lifts his head up from the table. "Can we at least have some music?"

"Yeah," Bill says. "How bout we crank up some tunes?!"

Greg nods his head but doesn't make a move toward the radio, That's Bill's territory.

"Okay, Bill, but not too loud," Karen insists.

Bill just shakes his head. He stands up, steps over, and sits down at the table with the radio, always happy to get away from the rest of us crazies. He turns it on and scans the dial until he finds an old classic rock song, Bruce Springsteen's *Baby We Were Born to Run*. He turns up the volume, "This is a great song. I'm gonna run the hell outta this crazy place!"

"Bill! Volume down, please," Karen says.

"Oh, Jesus!" Bill protests, then reluctantly lowers it.

I grab the black oil crayon and just start drawing furiously. I'm seeing something I want to capture, the crazy zigzag light and shadow patterns on a cracked-up canyon floor, kinda like how I feel. This gets Greg's attention. He seems to like the approach and picks up the green crayon.

"That just looks like a big ol' mess," Koran says to me.

Jane grabs her walker and edges her way over. "That doesn't look like a painting to me," she says.

"It's gonna look like crap!" Bill says from across the room. Then he smiles, "Yeah, let's draw some crap. That oughta make the docs happy!" He comes over, grabs a paper and purple crayon, and scribbles away.

"I think that it's all going to look very good," Ahmad mumbles as he picks up a blue oil crayon and starts making jagged lines on his paper

"Jackson's doing a great job of expressing himself. Don't worry about what it looks like," Karen says. "Just try to express how you're feeling. Try to see what you can express."

I grab the red oil crayon and add a bunch of jagged lines, spin my construction paper around, grab the purple and yellow oil crayons and keep on drawing away like a madman. Jane picks up the green crayon and Koran the pink one, and they both start drawing. Greg stands up, starts pulling his hair, grabs another crayon and keeps on drawing. As if on cue, the song from the band Heart, *Crazy on You*, comes on, with the chorus line, "Let me go *crazy, crazy* on you!"

"This is too perfect!" Bill says, steps over, and turns it up. The therapist lets it slide.

We're all drawing like madmen now. I'm tearing through crayons and my construction paper is coming *alive*. We go on like this for a couple more songs. Suddenly, Jennifer, the intern, walks into the group room. Watching all of this intense activity, she says, "Oh my god, you guys, what is going on here?"

"We're painting crap!" Greg yells.

She walks around the table looking at our wild and erratic paintings, but unlike the therapist, she is thrilled by what she sees. "This is amazing! These are *so* good!"

"You think so? Is you crazy too?" Koran asks.

"Yes! Koran, yours looks like the most intense Valentine card I've ever seen. And Jackson. Yours is *wonderful*! Such vibrant colors! So primal," she coos, almost red-faced. This makes me blush as well.

"Oooh," Jane says, smiling. "Someone likes you, Jackson."

Jennifer blushes even more.

Bill shakes his head at this remark, while Greg is drawing so ferociously that he's almost sweating.

"Okay guys, that was great! I'm really proud of all of your efforts," Karen says. "Let's start cleaning up."

"Wait a minute!" Jennifer shouts. "Do you mind if I use these paintings in an art-as- therapy show I'm putting together in Berkeley? They'll be kept anonymous, of course." Everyone smiles like they all just got gold stars. "Of course," she continues, "unless you want to keep yours." Everyone shakes their heads vehemently, No.

"If you think they good enough, you can have them for your crazy ass art show," Koran says, and everyone laughs.

"I think that mine is bery good," Ahmad adds.

Bill walks around the table. "They don't suck nearly as bad as I thought they would."

"You crazy Jackson," Koran says.

Jennifer now goes around and collects the drawings. She stops and stares at mine, and then writes on the bottom right corner of the painting, **JS** for Jackson Smith. "You don't mind, do you?"

"No, it's about time I take responsibility for my insanity."

Jennifer smiles. "Oh, Jackson, you're no more insane than the rest of the world."

The therapist now clears her throat. Jennifer picks up my drawing, adds it to her pile, and walks away. I watch her sashay out of the group room. Nice butt.

19.

My big, sad roommate was placed in the GTU (General Treatment Unit) in the next ward over. I don't think that he could summon enough energy to kill himself, so they moved him to the other, less restrictive ward. People from this ward are transferred to the GTU when they are deemed healthier, functional, or no longer a threat to themselves or others. Then their bed is filled by someone new, someone who's usually in real trouble. If you're not critical, like a suicide case, when you are admitted, they take you straight to the GTU. The worse off you are the longer you stay on this ward. I've been here for three weeks now. Dr. Canter says I'm making progress, but she still doesn't "trust" me and neither do I. The new doc might change her diagnosis.

Night comes and it's nice to have the room to myself for once. I did wonder if the demons might show up and party, but I guess they were busy doing something else.

The next morning, I wake up more refreshed. It makes me wonder if my old roomy wasn't draining my energy. Like he was saving up all his for when he got out of here, and just stealing all of mine while he was in here! What a prick! Light now streams in through the window and hits me in the face. Another day. I snap out of my negative spin-cycle.

The new, obese, sixty-two-year-old woman on the ward keeps yelling for her husband, her daughter and her daddy.

"Bill, Bill, Bill! Daddy . . . Daddy . . . Daddy! I can't breathe! I can't breathe! I can't breathe! Tracy, Tracy! Tracy!" Her room is right across from mine, and she's driving me nuts with her squawking. Maybell is so big that she can hardly walk. She looks like she hasn't left her house in twenty or thirty years. She's covered in sores and warts. Her pale, dead skin hasn't seen the sun in forever and just hangs off her dead lifeless body. Huge sickly bags of spoil lay rotting under her eyes—a face that shows how miserable life can get. Apparently, her mind is rotted, her soul warped. This is what life has done to her, or what she's allowed. Again, it makes me wonder what I'm doing here. By comparison I'm "well-adjusted."

"Tracy, Tracy, Tracy! . . . That's my bird, Tracy, please? . . . Pick up the bird for me! . . . Pick up the goddamn bird for me!" she yells over and over again.

Ahmad comes into my room, shaking his head.

"How do you write with all these noise?" he asks in his thick Middle Eastern accent. I look up. "Quit with the writing. I have to tell you something important. Walk down the hall with me! Come!"

I close my journal and stand up. Maybe he's going to tell me "the meaning of life?"

We walk up and down the hallway past the patient rooms, the nurses' station, and the group room. It's about 120 paces to the end of the ward. We faintly hear the new old woman's desperate voice echoing down the hall. "Tracy! . . . Tracy! Please!" Ahmad is silent, his eyes drifting as though deep in thought. Through the windows, I see that it's foggy out again. The ward smells like rotten vegetables, and my mind wanders to what Ahmad could be thinking is so important. I'm distracted by Bill yelling at the nurses' station from the group room.

"Won't she ever shut the hell up! Can't you shut her door or sometin'? And tell that bitch to stop yelling my name!"

One of the nurses tells him, "Bill, you know we can't shut people's doors."

"Jesus! She's drivin' me *fuckin* crazy! She ain't gonna try ta kill herself! Just shut her damn door!"

"Sorry, Bill. No can do. Just try to tune it out." The nurse now holds up a syringe and taps it. Bill gets the message. (Real subtle).

I look back at Ahmad hopefully. I could really use some insight about now. But it always surprises me when he says anything at all. Most of the time his thoughts are racing, his eyes are rolled up into the top of his head, and he mumbles to himself as he walks—his therapy. All of a sudden, he asks, "Do you ever want to get married?"

I turn to him surprised. "I don't know. Why, what do you think?" I ask him as the huge old woman yells in the background, "My bird! My bird! My bird! TRACY! Where's my bird?" I'd hate to be Tracy. Probably why she had the old lady committed, I think to myself.

Ahmad says in his thick Middle Eastern accent, "Don't get married if you're sick. I'm divorced. And don't have kids . . . A big mistake!"

"Thanks Ahmad, I'll try to remember that."

He nods his head approvingly, rubs his beard and looks up and out the windows toward the fog, stops talking and goes back to mumbling to himself. His thoughts are racing, broken, and he's too beaten down to think coherently. I'm a bit disappointed.

After lunch Koran stands outside my door—we're not supposed to go into other people's rooms—and asks me, "Is you really gonna come to visit me when you get outta here?"

I look up from my journal. "Of course, Koran."

"You a perfectly good-looking white boy, Jackson. I don't know what's wrong with you. Why you even here."

"Thanks, Koran, I don't know either. Maybe I just needed a vacation from life."

She laughs. "You crazy, Jackson! This a horrible place for a vacation! Come on now. Come outta dat room." I put my journal aside again. I'm never going to finish it here. But Koran is in charge now. She tells me what to do.

We sit in the group room and play checkers. She lets me win to help boost my confidence. We play *Sorry*, the board game where you try to move your pawns around the board while other players impede your progress and say "sorry." Seems like a perfect psych ward game or a metaphor for life. I win again. Afterward Koran has me retrieve my journal, and we sit together at one of the tables in the group room while I write after she's boosted my self-esteem by simply letting me win the board games. She supervises, giving me advice on what to write as she walks around the room cleaning up and putting things away, while talking nonstop and moving, always moving. The sun has come out a little. Ahmad comes back and tells us that his brain is on fire and has been for the past ten years. Koran suggests that he get some Tylenol 3 or Codeine from the nurses' station.

"That stuff will relax the muscles, stop the brain from bangin' against the skull," she says. Koran then yells at the nurses' station, "But don't nobody know that around here!" She breaks out into her great laugh and I can't help but laugh too. Even Ahmad smiles, as he walks over to get his Tylenol. Afterward he and Koran start walking up and down the hall together. Maybe he'll tell her the

meaning of life.

20.

A new shift of nurses just came on after breakfast this morning.

They have to change the shifts often, otherwise I think they'd decide

we weren't worth the effort and just let us all die. The head nurse

and some of the older ones remain.

The intercom crackles, "Group Time."

In group Bill asks if someone can shut the old lady up who

keeps shouting his name. He then tells the therapist how she is

ruining his recovery/vacation. As he's complaining, the old woman

yells in the background, "Daddy! DADDY! Where's my bird,

Tracy? Tracy!"

"*See!* That's exactly what I'm talkin about!" Bill says. "She's

drivin me batshit crazy! I can't take this!" He jumps up and storms

off to his room, slamming his door. The new mousy therapist with

tortoise shell glasses, a sensible blouse and beige nurse's shoes,

looks around the room like a kid who's lost her mom. What is she supposed to do now? The head nurse yells out to Bill, "You better open that door, Bill."

"The Hell I am!"

The mousy therapist looks around the room as though she still hasn't found her mother. "Okay, I think that's it for today," she says unconvincingly.

After group it's snack time. One of the nurses goes to Bill's door and tells him, "It's snack time; the cookies are going fast." Bill opens his door and steps out smiling. Cookies, fruit, juice, and milk are served. Bill comes over and tears into the snacks.

After snack time, it's afternoon reflection time. I skip this session. Writing in my journal is enough reflection for me.

In my room, I sit writing and recall an episode at school when someone beat up Aaron, and I yell out, "Son of bitch!" This apparently disturbs my new roommate who's already pretty disturbed. He looks like an old scarecrow with pale skin and white hair. He makes a cross in the air over his chest. He must be a Catholic-Protestant. The man just stares back at me because he can only mumble without any teeth. So, I pull out the Christian literature that Steven gave me, and I hold it out to him as a peace offering. He mumbles approvingly as he reads over it nonstop for thirty minutes or so, nodding his head and looking up at me from time to time.

After a while he pulls his chair next to me, looks at me and starts mumble-ranting. He goes on like this for a half hour or so moving his hands wildly in the air as he tells me his story. I catch bits and pieces of what he's saying—something about war, a divorce, children, and things that mean a lot to him but nothing to me, except that we all have our problems and eventually we all suffer. I don't know what to say. There's nothing I can tell him that would help. All I can do is sit and listen because I don't want to hurt his feelings, and *someone* has to listen to a schizophrenic, sixty-five-year-old nice madman with no teeth, right? He slipped out of reality and lost his life.

He keeps me awake most of the night mumbling to himself with his head in his hands sitting on the edge of his bed, occasionally getting up to pace the room or to speak into the intercom on the wall above my bed that he no doubt believes is connected to God. He opens the drapes, laughs, turns on the lights, then looks through the drawers. Always with the drawers.

I wake up at around 3:00 in the morning to find him standing by the sink, naked, laughing to himself and drying his crotch with my towel. I make a note to get a new towel first thing tomorrow and then another note not to let myself forget when I fall back asleep...And I think to myself how crazy my life here has become, and I doze off.

The next morning Steven calls me—he calls Koran and me almost every day. He says he wants to come back to the hospital. Severely depressed again. Still. But his insurance won't cover the cost.

He says over the phone, in his kind of whining, droning voice, ". . . The Catholic College where I was going to school Jackson, before I came to the hospital, refused to reaccept me. They kicked me out." School was his safety net and now he's left untethered.

"I'm sorry, Steven," I sympathize.

"It's lonely out here, Jackson. "I'm sad and I don't know what to do anymore."

"I'll come see you when I get out, Steven. You'll figure it out."

"You promise, Jackson?"

"I promise."

After I hang up, I walk up and down the hallway to shake off his desperation vibe. As I look around the ward, the sheer planned monotony of the hospital and its routines becomes obvious. I have to leave. I'm not crazy, or not like these people. Life is insane, and more so here in this *fucking* place. The longer I'm here the more I give into this madness. I just don't care enough, or maybe I care too much, like my doctor says and that's why I just shut myself off, because life was too much, too absurd, too insane and it's just easier to block it out, to not care anymore. Dr. Canter may be right because the sad thing is that I really do want to live, live fully, and not give in to the pathetic, meaningless existence that has become my life here. I want to love someone so much it hurts *again*. I want to scream in the desert again! I want to remember what it feels like to be in love with life *again*!

I walk up to the nurses' station and ask for an appointment with Dr. Canter. The nurse looks at her schedule. Makes a call and tells me she'll see me after lunch. I can't wait. Later, I step into her office.

"Take a seat, Jackson," Dr. Canter says, glancing up from her computer screen.

I sit down on the weathered couch, underneath the dream catcher, wishing I had a bigger dream than just getting out of this loony bin. She leans back in her chair, looking at me as if to imply, 'This better be good. I'm busy, and I've had enough crazy shit for one day.' I know I have to choose my words carefully if I want her to release me back into the wild, I have to be honest with her too.

"So, you wanted to see me. What's up?"

I take a deep breath, compose myself. "Yes," I say. "I've had some realizations, while journaling, about myself and my life."

"Okay," she says, her brow furrowing a bit, a slight smile crossing her lips.

"I've been thinking back to how this all started and why Aaron meant so much to me." I lean forward on the couch. There's a lump in my throat. "I don't know why it's so difficult to talk about all this."

"It's okay," Canter says empathetically, "Just tell me what you're thinking."

"Well, this all goes back to before I met Aaron. I mean, if I'm honest, I was feeling really uncomfortable in my own skin back in high school, worried all the time about what everyone was thinking of me, and the high expectations that my parents had for me, and not having a clue what I really wanted for myself. And then I met Aaron, and he seemed so unconcerned with what *anyone* thought. Like he didn't really give a shit, be it students or teachers. And I liked that, because I wanted to feel that confident... *free.*"

"I can see its appeal for you, Jackson. But that kind of devil-may-care attitude can be a slippery slope. I'm sure you can see that."

"Yeah, I guess. I mean, I slid down pretty far." I pause a moment as scenes from Aaron's car crash arise. I close my eyes to readjust. "But it wasn't just that he was wild. He also had the guts to say things that other people were afraid to say, even though they were probably thinking it, and wanted to say it, and things that probably *needed* to be said. He would tell anyone what he thought, anytime. And he would laugh when people tried to attack him. He would *laugh* at their insults."

"Would he insult people?"

"No, not really. He'd usually just walk away, because he didn't really care."

I thought about that attitude and how it cuts both ways.

"What are you thinking, Jackson?" Dr. Canter asks.

"Well, I guess that's why Aaron is dead. He died because of his fuck-it-all and burn-it-to-the-ground attitude."

Dr. Canter looks at me intently. "That's what I've been waiting for you to get at," she says. "But that's not all of it, is it?" She looks at me inquisitively.

"No. It isn't . . . I don't really hear Aaron's voice. Do I?"

"Of course, you don't." She says, then pauses. "You've just been processing your grief."

Tears start to pool, I lean back into the couch and look up at the painting of the shirtless Indian on the horse, arms reaching out skyward, asking for a revelation. And I laugh. I burst out laughing, loud and hard, leaning forward on the couch, rubbing my hands together as though I've just figured something out. "I'm not crazy!" I say. I look at Dr. Canter. "I'm just trying to figure out who the hell I am without Aaron."

Dr. Canter nods her head and leans over her desk. I'm sure if she were on my side, she'd take my hand, despite her "rules."

"I mean, some of the people here are *really* crazy and probably don't have a shot in hell at living a real life. And I guess I'm tired of wasting the life that I've been given, even if that sounds corny."

"First of all. I'm glad to hear you say that Jackson," Canter says. "Some clichés have an element of truth, and that's why they are repeated. And of course, you're not crazy. But you have been very confused and sad for a while now. That can happen when life throws us terribly painful events. We falter, but that's a part of life that everyone has to deal with. And, sorry to say, you're going to experience a lot more of these downturns throughout the rest of your life."

I nod my head. "Yeah. I kind of figured."

"And the thing is, you're not going to be able to control a lot of the difficult things that life will throw at you. But you can control how you respond to it. *That* is the trick to this recovery. I'm going to give you a book entitled, *Man's Search for Meaning*, by Victor Frankel. He survived the World War II concentration camps and suffered immensely. And he says that the only thing that saved him, that kept him sane, was realizing that the *only* thing that the Nazis couldn't control was how he reacted to his situation. How you react to the situations that life presents you are what will define you. And I'm willing to bet, Jackson, that if you put yourself out there, and care about yourself and others, and pursue things that interest you, life will respond to you in no small measure."

"Let's hope so," I say sincerely. I could use some help from "out there."

"If you look at this stint as a learning experience, you will grow. I've seen you grow in empathy and compassion for some of the hard cases here. That's something that a lot of people will never know, compassion for the afflicted. But," she says forcefully, "you need some direction."

"I know I do."

"Do you want to know what I think?"

"No, but at this point, I could use some guidance."

"Okay. You seem to like writing in your journal, don't you?"

"Yeah. I guess I do. I find it comforting. I've been pretending that I'm writing a story about someone else's life."

"Okay. That's good. And what is this person learning? What is he seeing?"

"It's being slowly *revealed* to him that he's been using his dead friend to avoid dealing with his issues and do the one thing that he really doesn't want to do."

"Which is what?" Dr. Canter asks, leaning back in her chair and smiling as though she's sincerely impressed with this development.

"Well, he has to grow up; I mean that I have to grow up. And it sucks. But there's really no other choice, other than more suffering, or maybe dying in a fiery car crash high on drugs like Aaron."

"So," she says flatly, sitting forward, looking directly in my eyes as though she's scanning my soul, "does the character in your story still have thoughts of suicide."

I think about this briefly, but without too much hesitation. "No. He made a commitment to God, or to the Great Buffalo in the Sky, or *whatever,* to live his life as fully as possible and try to see it all as a crazy adventure, and that by doing that it would be the best way to honor his dead friend."

"Okay." Dr. Canter says, nodding her head. "I think this story will have a decent ending.

You should keep journaling, and more will be revealed. It will give you the direction you're looking for." She looks down at her book, makes a note, then looks up. "So, tomorrow we'll move you to the GTU ward, as the first stage of your transition back into the world." Dr. Canter stands up. "I'm proud of you, Jackson. You're going to be a great success story."

I smile. "I hope so."

21.

I am assigned a room in the General Treatment Unit. My old roommate, like me, was suffering from depression, but the drugs seem to have helped him. He's still a bit introverted and doesn't talk much. But that's good. I need to focus on myself. The therapy sessions here are less about recovery and more about adjustment to the outside world. I don't think that they have a cure for my *demons*, and I don't bring *them* up as I don't want to return to the ICU ward. I'll just have to deal with them on my own terms. I'm not afraid of them anymore. They just stand over my bed at night now and then, dark shadows watching me. And when I pray to God, then they're

gone. I feel better than I have in a long time, but I still feel an

indefinable emptiness that I'm not sure anything or anyone can ever

cure.

This morning I have my first group session in the GTU. The

sun is shining today. I feel anxious, like a hornet's nest has been

released in my stomach.

There's only three of us in our discharge group: Me. A

woman in her sixties who looks fairly well adjusted, just a little tired

and resigned, and a blond-haired girl in her twenties. Her hair is

pulled back into a ponytail and her knees pulled up into her chest,

her arms wrapped tightly around them as though protecting herself

from the outside world.

"Okay," the therapist with graying hair starts. A clipboard

rests on her lap, and she has a steely look in her eyes like she's seen

it *all.* "What are some of your biggest concerns about being

discharged?" she asks, then scans the group with a 'don't try to

bullshit me' look. "Kay," she says looking at the fifty year old. "You

start."

"Okay." Kay says. "I guess I'm worried that I'm alone. My children are in other cities, married with families of their own. My husband, my ex I should say, is remarried. My only friend is the neighbor who I've been drinking with." She pauses. "I don't consider her a real friend. And I don't think that she wants to stop drinking."

"Kay brings up some good points," the therapist says. "Support on the outside is important. And most people leaving here, especially when we don't have close family and friends, have to find new support groups." The sun is glaring in my eyes, and I kind of drift off, as the therapist continues on about AA meetings and outpatient groups. Then my mind starts to go fuzzy like the static screen on a television set. "And we need to stay on our medications. And what else?"

She looks around the group but no takers. "Therapy and meditation, breathing exercises, physical exercise, and good nutrition." My mind goes blank white for a second as I picture riding my BMX as a kid, the wind blowing through my hair as I raced along the dirt trail near my house, not a care in the world. "Places we can go," she says and drones on in the background, "and things that we can do away from people who are drinking or doing drugs—self-medicating, in other words." Again, my eyes are wet with tears and I can't swallow because of the lump in my throat. 'It's all going to be okay.' I tell myself. "Find places where we can make healthy, happy, and positive new friends. And don't forget the importance of journaling and praying." I remember the fort that the BMX trail through the woods that lead to where we had a hideout with porno mags and a small bottle of whisky. I remember the strange feeling seeing the pictures in the magazine, the burning in my throat and stomach from the whisky, then the buzzing feeling in my head.

"Jackson," the therapist says, snapping me back into the present, to the feeling of uncertainty pervading my mind. "What are your main concerns?"

I think for a second, try to focus. "All of it." The therapist gives me a sour look. "I mean, I need to do everything you pointed out, all that stuff." She nods her head unconvincingly.

She now turns to the blond-haired girl. "And then there's sexual abstinence." The girl pulls her legs together and sighs.

Later, coming back from a session with Dr. Canter in ICU, I spot Koran in the group room. We sit down together and play checkers and talk. She has an orange for me. She knows the medication dries my mouth out. This kindness makes me feel warm inside.

"I'm gonna miss you, Jackson. They say they're lettin' me out of here next week," Koran says.

"You don't have to come to the GTU?"

"Probly not 'til you gone. I still don' know why you wanted to kill yourself." She shakes her head.

"I think I was just tired of everything." She laughs at this lame excuse. "You're gonna see me again, Koran. I'm gonna come and visit you when we're out."

"Okay, Jackson, if you say, but I live in a pretty rough neighborhood," she says, but I can tell she doesn't believe me.

"You're an all-right guy, after all," Bill says to me as he steps over to the snack table—four bags of Graham Crackers and four cartons of milk. "I don't care if I never leave this place! But good luck to ya," he says grinning from ear to ear. "Hey, how's the food over there? Is it any better than here?"

"No. It's pretty much the same."

"Damn. I was thinkin' a movin' over 'cause they don't got any crazies there. That old bat callin' my name all the time is drivin' me crazy."

"Yeah, same for me. It's hard to get well when you can't get any sleep."

"Ain't dat da truth." He looks at me sort of smiling. "Remember, life's a bitch buddy, and everyone's out to screw ya! Best a luck! And don't come back, or I'll beat the shit out of ya." He laughs as if he thinks that's the funniest thing anyone ever said.

Dr. Canter says at our next session that it's imperative that I have a plan. "You also need some structure and some help right now," she says from behind her big oak desk. She says that she has been working out a plan with my parents. They've been in constant communication about me and she's had me check in with them lately, or with my mom. Dad never seems to be around.

"We know you've had a rough time," my mom said to me last night over the phone, "and we're not upset about the money anymore (the money that I blew on my suicide trip), and we're proud of you. Your doctor says you've resolved some of your issues, and she seems hopeful for your future. You've got so much potential, Jackson. It's hard on us seeing you waste it. I know you and Aaron had some crazy plan to go to Ecuador or wherever and become surfers. But that's not realistic, Jackson. It never was. It's time to get serious about your future."

"I know, Mom. I've been talking to Dr. Canter about all of that. I'm ready to go to college and get a real job and think about my future."

"You know your father and I will help support you in moving forward with your life. But you have to take this seriously. What are you planning on studying?"

"I'm thinking of studying writing."

"You mean get a degree in English? That's almost as useless as learning how to surf."

"There's nothing else I'm really interested in. Grandpa got a degree in English. He writes."

"He writes as a hobby. And he worked hard all his life as an English teacher, because that's about all you can do with an English degree, and he and your grandmother always struggled financially."

"I think, as Dr. Carter says, I need to first find something that motivates me."

"No matter for now, at least you're going to move forward." She paused for a moment.

"Well, there's one more thing I need to tell you. Your grandparents have had to move into a nursing home. The house was just too much for them to maintain."

I sigh. "I'm sorry, Mom. I feel bad," I say, feeling somehow responsible, like I let them down. One more thing I failed at.

"It's okay, Jackson. They're old. It was inevitable. Also, that very nice gay man, Charlie, who was helping them out, picked up your car from the motel and took it to your grandparents' house. He put the key on the back tire."

"Wow. Really? That's great. I hadn't even thought of that."

Mom grunted, and I could just see her shaking her head. "Your'e going to have to start paying your own car insurance soon. I truly hope you're out of the woods and have your head on straight now. You're being given another chance in life, and you need to make good on that."

"I will Mom."

"Let's hope so. Dr. Canter believes you can do well, and we're willing to pay your tuition at the Community College and your rent at the halfway home. That is, as long as you go to your out-patient program, get yourself a job, and pay the rest of your bills."

I look around the ward at the other patients walking around in pill stupors with thousand-yard stares of hurt, sadness, loneliness, and confusion. I've got to do that because I can't take this craziness any longer.

"I can do that, Mom."

"Good then. Your father sends you his love. And we're sorry we couldn't make it out there to see you, but we've been incredibly busy with work. Maybe we could fly you home for Christmas if you're up to it."

"Let's see, Mom."

"And, have Dr. Canter tell us the address of the halfway house, and we'll Western Union you some money somewhere nearby so you can get on your feet."

"Thanks, Mom."

"You're welcome. Do you have enough money for the bus fare to go and get your car?"

"Yeah, I still have a little money left. Nothing to spend it on here."

"Okay. Call us tomorrow and let us know that you're okay. We love you."

"I love you too."

My doctor and my parents feel good about the prospect of my future, and it's been decided after a couple days in GTU that I'm checking out today.

Dr. Canter says, "Besides everything else, you'll also be enrolled in an Intensive Outpatient Program here at the hospital that you'll need to attend three days a week for three hours a day. The halfway house has five other guys living there. It's a mix of guys between 18 and 30. Some are struggling with sobriety. Some with mood disorders like you. Some both. You'll be expected to stay sober too. How does that sound to you?"

"Sounds good. I'm just a little worried about the halfway house."

"That's understandable. But I really think it will be good for you to be around other guys who are struggling with the same, or similar issues. Does that make sense to you?"

I nod my head a little hopeful, and somewhat resigned to my fate.

"You'll be fine Jackson, and we'll talk next week at our Outpatient session."

Not long after lunch, one of the nurses comes into my room holding a clear plastic bag of pills and some paperwork.

"Here are your medications," she says, setting the bag on my bed. "It's enough to get you through the rest of the month." She looks down, and I get the impression that she's not quite as hopeful about my future as Dr. Canter. "Now, let's go over your discharge plan."

"Okay," I say, a bit nervous and suddenly unsure about my discharge.

"You'll be going to outpatient three times a week and seeing Dr. Canter once a week. You'll be staying in a halfway house in Oakland. I've included the BART train schedule from Oakland to here if you need it. I've talked with the Community College and had your high school transcript emailed to them. The admission's officer was impressed and especially with your IQ test score. Her contact information is also included. In so far as getting a job, that's pretty much up to you. I might add that you're not required by law, unless it's a police or military job, to add to job applications about your hospitalization. Just say you recently moved here after high school."

I give this nurse another onceover. She's pretty efficient, if not hopeful.

"Does that sound right to you?" she asks, now looking me in the eyes.

"Yes. And I'll put makeup on my slit wrist mark." This kind of startles her.

She now laughs. "Jackson, you seem to get the gist of this better than most."

I nod my head, but despite her encouragement, I feel a tremor of anxiety shoot through me, creating a knot in my stomach. My mouth is dry. I don't want to live in a halfway house or here, but I don't want to go back home either.

"Okay, then, I just need you to sign these forms." She hands me the papers and a pen.

"Your things are ready for you by the nurses' station." And just like that I stepped out into my *Brave New World*. I wonder if they have camera surveillance?

PART III

22.

I picked up my car after I got out...I felt like a stranger sitting behind the wheel that day. I drove so carefully, methodically. Focused on the road more closely than ever before. Aware of the beauty of the city around me for the first time.

I've been out of the hospital for a week, living in a halfway house. The house is supposed to be sober living quarters, but I'm pretty sure that Brock and Trevor, the head honchos drink. As such, they probably let the other two guys slide. The only sober ones are me and my roommate, as we're fresh out of the hospital. The house has three bedrooms with two beds in each, for a total of six guys. My roommate, Jason, is a little younger than me, kind of quiet and shy. The two oldest guys, Brock and Trevor, who are somewhere in their late 20s, run the house. The guys here seem to give each other a little bit of space and understanding as we're all dealing with shitty situations. We do need to keep the place clean, and every so often a guy from the company who owns the house comes over and checks to make sure we're not ruining their investment. And I was told there are spot drug tests, but I don't think they really enforce it. Either way, I'm going to try to keep myself straight.

The house is in a working-class neighborhood somewhere between Berkeley and Oakland. Ours is by far the worst-looking house on the street of small squat houses of different shades of grey and in various states of dilapidation. The lawns are unkempt, and a couple of the houses have cars on blocks in the driveway or on the lawn. But the neighborhood is quiet and has its fair share of trees, and people seem to keep to themselves. They don't bother us. I was told a few of our past "residents" cracked open the heads of a couple of intruders once, so the word got out—don't mess with the crazy house.

There's not much near us of interest. If you walk in almost any direction to one of the main streets that connect Berkeley and Oakland, all you'll find are rundown shops, bars, grocery stores and a few crackheads and drunks here and there. It's not that exciting a location, probably by design. No place to get in real trouble. At least it's not a ghetto with hookers hanging out on the corners. I guess it's as good a place as any to sort out my life and move forward. I like being out of the hospital and away from all the real crazies, even if I have to go back for group sessions. And I like having some freedom and watching sports on TV or turn-your-brain-off action-adventure movies with the other guys. Mike, who's all tatted up used to work in a restaurant, so he cooks dinners and the rest of us clean up and wash the dishes.

I've signed up for a couple of summer classes at the community college. I need to start looking for a job, but some days I just can't get out of bed. I'm attending the day program back at the hospital three times a week—we have more intensive discussions, therapy sessions, and meetings. After being around "normal" people in the neighborhood and at the local pool hall, being cooped up for hours with a bunch of troubled guys makes me feel kind of freaked out. Supposedly, I'm gaining *something* that I need, but have yet to figure out what that is. It's so depressing being around people all the time who can't get their lives together. I have to get my own life back on track and upgrade my social group. The meetings are in the basement of the hospital that smells like stale coffee, smoke, and desperation. The walls are a pale sick-green illuminated by glaring fluorescent lights. Of course, I can relate to some of their adjustment issues, but nobody (including the therapists) seem to have any answers.

Everything in my life just seems like a slow blur or a copy of a copy of a copy. Maybe it's the medication? I'm not sure. Everything just appears before me like scenes from a movie about someone else's dismal life. So, I guess this is the part in the story where the guy goes off to college to make his way in the world? But it all feels somehow too contrived to me, like a tired script meant for somebody else and I miss Aaron and the thought of adventure, even if I no longer want to hear his voice.

I sit sometimes in the front window, staring out at the rain, thinking about my new life. Honestly I feel kind of lonesome. I take my medication. I pace back and forth on the porch. I smoke and try to tune out the thoughts telling me that my life is fucked, that I should just end it all, or hop a freight train, but to where? I am fine, or will be fine, I tell myself rather unconvincingly. But my new resolve or my recent revelations about getting on with my life seems to have evaporated. Today the rain falls, and the outside world looks even bleaker. I know I've got to get a job. School starts soon, where I will meet people and have to fit in, or so I hope, or do I? I'm lucky my parents love me, have given me money to get settled. Lucky I don't have to live in a halfway house in the ghetto like Koran, or in the basement of my mom's house like Steven. My hands shake, and I have trouble pissing because of the medication. In the morning I watch the scantily clad girls walking by on the sidewalk outside in gaggles, on their way to high school or college or work. One day I try to masturbate when my roommate is out, but it's difficult to cum. It's all pretty pathetic and I feel like I need a girlfriend. Good luck with that.

I'll be okay, I tell myself repeatedly.

It's Monday again.

The rain falls harder, and I pull the folded wad of paper out of my wallet with the telephone number to Koran's halfway house, and I dial the number.

"Hello," a stern-sounding woman's voice on the other end of the says.

"I'm calling for Koran. Is she staying there?"

"Can I ask who's calling?" the woman says with a hint of suspicion in her voice.

"My name is Jackson. I know her from the hospital."

"Okay, hold on just a minute." I hear her shuffling through papers. "Okay, she says . . . Koran put you on her contact list. Just a second." She puts the phone down, and I hear her call out over the faint crackling of the phone, "Has anyone seen Koran? Koran! Phone! Someone tell Koran, phone!" I hear her great laugh in the background, and something *lights* up inside of me. I hear the patter of footsteps approaching. "Phone's for you, dear!" the nurse says.

"Jackson, that *really* you? . . . I knew you were gonna call! . . . You better come get me tomorrow?"

"Of course, I can. I got my car back." I think about how lucky I am to have a car and how sad it was to go to my grandparents' house and have the house be dark and empty, void of their light and love. And I feel bad for not going to see them yet at the old-age home.

"Okay. I can leave for two hours in the afternoon. You come and get me tomorrow at 2:00! Is that late enough for you? I know you don't like gettin up early. You come and get me now, you hear?"

"Okay, Koran. I'll be there tomorrow at 2:00."

"You promise?" she asks. Sounds unsure of things.

"Promise."

"See you then, White Boy."

23.

The next day the sun is out, and I find Koran's halfway house just off the highway in the bad part of town, broken down buildings with trash in the street. It's a tall white building, skeletal, on the corner. Empty lots surround it. Even though the surroundings are trashy, everything seems a little brighter to me, almost too bright, surreal. Maybe it's the sun? Maybe it's because I'm going to see the vivacious and always entertaining Koran? The air feels sharper. My thoughts feel quicker, almost frenzied, and I wonder if it's the medication, or my "Spidey sense" tingling, as I park the car and go inside. I push through the glass front doors. I hit the elevator button to the eighth floor, but it doesn't work, and I have to climb the eight flights of stairs.

I open the staircase doors to an all white hallway, dirty linoleum floors, white walls. A nurse's desk is at the end of the hall where I see Koran waiting patiently for me. She smiles brightly when she sees me coming down the hall. Her hair is straight and stiff, like a wig, framing her gleaming face.

"Jackson!" she says, "I been waitin' on you! Come on now, sign me out, so we can get goin! We don't got that long. And I can't take this place no more!" She smirks at the nurse who hands me a pen and asks me for my ID, telling me that I'm responsible for Koran and need to have her back by 4:00 this afternoon. As I hand the nurse my ID, she eyes me suspiciously, inspecting my face like a detective as she takes down my information.

"Come on now, let's go," Koran says, as she grabs my arm and turns toward the nurse. "Let's get the hell out of this place!" The nurse smiles at Koran, walks around past us and puts a key in the wall next to the call button that brings the elevator to our floor.

"I thought it was broken," I say.

Koran looks at me again like I'm crazy. "I done told you, you gotta call from the phone downstairs to get the elevator, but you don't listen to nothin!" The two of them laugh at this remark.

It's warm out and the sky is a vibrant pale blue. A free-floating anxiety hovers heavy in the air over my entire being.

"Where do you want to go?" I ask Koran, as we walk through the dirty parking lot toward my car.

"Damn, this a nice car Jackson," she says as I open the door for her.

"My parents bought it for me in High School. It's my cousin Braydon's old car." I walk around the back of the car feeling slightly disconnected from my life.

I climb in and roll the windows down. She looks over at me through the stale air of the car. "You lucky to have parents who love you the way yours do. You're a perfectly fine-looking White Boy. What the hell done happened to you?"

"I don't know, Koran."

"No, I guess you don't or you wouldn't a'been in the hospital then, would you?" she says, making us both break out laughing.

"Come on, let's go now. I needs to go somewhere to pick somethin' up," she tells me as I start the car up.

We weave through rundown neighborhoods with dead trees and abandoned cars, passing nothing but liquor stores, rundown convenience stores, and pawn shops until we come to a boarded-up house on a barren-looking street.

"Pull up here," Koran says, "and don't get outta the car for no one, for no reason. And stay down. You hear me?" I nod. "People will wonder what your white ass and clean car is doin' here. I'll be right back." She climbs out of the car and disappears quickly around the back of the house.

Nothing stirs on the blank street with dead lawns as I lay low.

Fifteen minutes later Koran comes back. I look at her.

"Lets go to tha park and smoke a joint. You know how to roll a joint, Jackson?" I turn and smile at her, look at her sideways out of my eyes, and she laughs.

"Okay, but just a couple hits for me. They supposedly drug test at my halfway."

"Jesus. That's worse than mine."

At the park we sit on some broken down aluminum bleachers near an abandoned baseball field surrounded by brown grass amongst a cluster of tall disfigured trees. I can hear the cars on the freeway passing close by. The skyline of Oakland rises abruptly in the distance. No one else is around.

"You gotta job yet?" Koran asks, as I pick the stems and seeds out of the weed feeling slightly uneasy in these surroundings.

"No. Not yet. I looked in the paper, but no ads for 'ex-crazies.'"

She laughs at this inside joke. "You're crazy, Jackson. But you *gotta* get one!"

"Yeah. I know. And I gotta go to school and straighten up."

She adds, "Well, soon as I get outta dis halfway house, I'm gonna get a job, probbly workin' at the grocery store." She hands me a rolling paper and I start clumsily rolling the joint. "You should go and visit Steven. He's real lonesome."

"Yeah. I know," I tell her. I picture Steven in his basement reading or walking around his neighborhood staring into the sky. I pass Koran the awkward-looking joint. I'm nervous about even taking a few hits on this medication. My stomach is a wound-up knot. Koran looks over at me, sensing my anxiety.

"Maybe we shouldn't be smoking any of this?" Koran says, looking at the sad joint that I've rolled. "I don't wanna be a bad influence on you. And I really wants to get myself together this time."

I tell her to light up the joint, that we'll be okay this once. She smiles, lights it, takes a couple of puffs and passes it to me as I look at the small plastic bag with what's left of the ragged looking weed. I take two puffs, the joint crackling as it burns red.

The sun glares overhead.

The joint smells like disinfectant or bleach or something.

I pass it back to her. "That's all for me." I look around. The trees are surrounded by an aura of energy that I hadn't noticed earlier. The air is filled with a deadly calm. The sun radiates. Something's wrong. Koran seems frozen in thought. I don't know how long we've been sitting in the silence. Everything's wrong. I feel electric and sick. My stomach churns. Purple lines trace the perimeter of the trees. The skyscrapers are looming ominously. Angry negative energy emanates from the surrounding neighborhoods as Koran speaks, her voice is distant and distorted.

"I think this stuff was laced with somethin'. I think it might be that Sherm. Embalmin' fluid . . ." Her voice trails off then rushes back as I take a deep breath fighting off panic surging through my body.

Deathly quiet.

"Shit . . ." I mutter. "I think someone killed all the birds in this neighborhood."
She glances at me skeptically, then smiles angelically and we both start laughing uncontrollably. "We shouldn'ta smoked that danm stuff . . . Damn ghetto weed! I'm sorry, Jackson! Let's get outta here. Take me back to tha halfway house, will ya?

My eyes are watering from laughing so hard. I need some Visine.

"I don't know if can drive right now, Koran."

"You'll be okay," she says, laughing. "Just focus on the road, and we'll both go home and take a nap and sleep this stuff off. We'll try again another day. Okay?"

"Yeah, let's get out of here."

I focus on the road and follow her directions past the bleak uninhabitable-looking buildings through neglected neighborhoods as I slowly and carefully make my way back to the parking lot of her halfway house.

I park and take a deep breath. I'm a bit high. Glad I didn't smoke more. I just want to get home and hide from the world. I write down my phone number for Koran.

"Are you gonna get in trouble for goin' in there stoned?" I ask her. Her eyes look a little red.

"Hell no!" she says as she gets outta the car. "They'll want some!" Before she closes the door, she turns to me. "Go home and get some rest Jackson and start looking for that job tomorrow!" She smiles. "I'll call and check on ya. Go on now," she says and closes the door. "Thanks for coming to see me . . ."

I weave my way home through the strange and foreign streets as the sun retreats. I get lost along the way, finally find my place and hide away and sleep.

24.

The next day, I feel a little out of it but walk through the streets, fog overhead, looking for work in a gentrifying neighborhood. I pass by clothing and record stores, Chinese restaurants, magazine shops, coffee shops, and bars. I try to picture a workplace that's a fit for me. Cars honk, people jostle each other, and the smell of Kung Pao fills the air. I try to act excited about the prospect of getting a job, about meeting people, making friends, earning some money. Being a productive member of society. As I walk along, I try to create in my mind a list of desirable working qualities and skills that I would put down on an application. My mind goes blank. The fog rolls in and I feel muddled.

I wander aimlessly past the uncaring and indifferent masses, ending up in a bookstore bathroom and staring at myself in the mirror in the glaring fluorescent white light. I ask myself, "who in the hell I am," staring endlessly at my beaten-down image while washing my hands raw in the sink, lost in this reflection. "Where do you fit in? What do you have to offer this world? Answer for yourself!" Tired of walking, tired of searching for a job, with no answers to my questions, I step back into the bookstore. I browse through the sections and come upon some art books. One is a retrospective of Jackson Pollock's work. I think back to our art therapy session and all the chaotic "Pollock" paintings we did. Then I think of Jennifer, the intern, which brings a smile to my face. I sit down and look through the book for hours. It helps.

On the way home, I see a sign in the window of a chain coffee shop: NOW HIRING: WILL TRAIN. I walk inside. The place feels slick and energetic, fast food coffee with catchy theme music and young, hip, smiling employees.

"What can I getcha?" asks one of the female baristas.

"Could I get a job application?" I ask.

She looks at me closely, undecided. "Sure. Hold on. I'll get the manager." She turns, fills a cup from a stainless-steel coffee dispenser, and hands it to me. "Here. Have a seat over there. He'll be right with you."

I add some cream from a corner kiosk and take a seat at one of the wooden tables by the large floor-to-ceiling windows that look out at the bustling street and the gray day.

"We need bodies ASAP," the young manager with bangs in his eyes tells me as he sits down at the table, putting an application between us. "We're really just looking for people with personality," he says, as he eyes me up and down. Seems a bit doubtful. "We can train the rest."

I need to make a good impression. "Well, I'm full of it, I mean personality, if you get my drift."

He smiles vaguely. Not a good time for a joke. *Stop talking*, I tell myself. But he does fill me in on possible job responsibilities and tells me a lot about coffee. Way *too* much. I just nod my head now and then, as if I give a crap.

"Well, that about covers everything, Jackson. Great name, by the way. Take this application, fill it out, and bring it back to me tomorrow if you're still interested."

When I get home, the house is empty. Everyone is at work. You have to have a job within thirty days of moving in or you get kicked out. I look over the application, thinking about my previous work experience: Hiding in a warehouse; Dumping people in a lake; Coloring pictures in the psych ward for Valentine's Day. *Shittt. How'm I gonna get a job?* The phone on the wall is blinking. I check it. There's a message from Koran asking me how the job hunt went and wishing me luck. "Show 'em your smile Jackson," her message says. "You gotta great smile!" I wonder if Koran is my Guardian Angel.

The sun has decided to come out and is annoyingly bright, and I'm pulsing nervous as I walk down the street to turn in my application. The coffee shop is glossy, vibrant, and a little too put-together. It's chaotic and noisy inside. There's a manufactured friendliness to the place that's a little annoying. But they're hiring. Inside, a line of customers reaches all the way to the door. The smell of coffee fills the air. Steam blows from the wands of the espresso machines as the employees bark out orders in an almost foreign-sounding language. It's the early rush hour, and it's obvious that they're understaffed. I feel ill at ease about the prospect of working here as I walk around the line looking for the manager. He's refilling one of the creamer dispensers. I step over and wait until he's finished.

He turns to me. Stares back. "Oh, yeah, Jackson. The new applicant."

I hand him my application and flash him an enthusiastic smile, "full of personality."

"Thank you," he says rather dryly, looking a little frazzled. "I'll look it over today. As you can see, we need bodies."

He turns and heads back to his office. I look around the shop and wonder if it's too hectic for me. Maybe a quiet bookstore would be a better fit, but who is hiring book clerks. But then, maybe I need a kick in the ass to jumpstart me back into life.

I'm in a daze as I head back to the halfway house. As I pass through the streets covered in old bubblegum, piss and the vacant-eyed homeless, I think of Steven. As soon as I get back, I call him. His mom answers.

"Hello, who's calling please?" She sounds suspicious.

"Is Steven there? This is Jackson. I knew him at the hospital."

"Jackson . . . Oh, okay, he told me about you. Hold on." I can hear footsteps and a door opening. She calls out, "Steven! Steven . . . Phone!"

I can hear Steven yelling in the background, "Who is it, Ma?"

"Your friend, Jackson!"

"Okay. I got it!" He picks up the phone. "Hang up, Ma!" I hear the line click. "Jackson? Is that really you?"

"Hey, yeah, it's me."

He asks tentatively, "How are you doing?"

"I'm good, really. Staying at a halfway house with a group of guys. I just applied for a job at a coffee shop," I say energetically, if unconvincingly.

"Oh, that's good Jackson. But how are you doing *mentally?*"

Trick question. "I'm hanging in there. The group sessions keep me in line."

"It's not enough. I think you need God, Jackson."

"Yeah, I know. Can you introduce me?" I say, a bit flatly.

He snorts. "Yeah, I can arrange an introduction. Can you come and get me this Sunday, and I'll take you to church with me? I've decided to be a Catholic again. I think God can do a lot for you Jackson."

I'm not sure if that's true, but I do need to connect with him. "Okay. That sounds good. I'll come get you. Got my car back."

"Good, Jackson. I think you'll like Father Howard. He's real, no bullshit. Runs a 12-step program at the church."

"Sounds good. And how are you doing, Steven?"

He pauses. "Oh, you know," he says in his slow drawl. "I think I need to go back in the hospital again. I've got nothing to live for. I can't go back to school. I don't have the money, they kicked me out anyway, and besides that the medication makes it hard for me to think clearly. I don't know what I'm gonna do. I'm hoping God will give me a sign."

"He's probably got a better handle on the 'Big Picture' than you do Steven."

"Yeah, you're right. I think meeting up will be good for both of us. I'm kinda at loose ends."

"I know what you mean. Even though I'm making the effort, I wonder if any of it will pan out."

He pauses for a long moment. "You mean the coffee shop?"

"Yeah, but who's gonna hire me anyhow?"

"I think you'll get it, Jackson. You're a nice guy, and you're smart. Pick up things quickly. That's what they want."

"Let's hope so."

"Okay, Jackson." He gives me his address. "I gotta go now. Pick me up at 9:00 Sunday morning.

I hang up the phone and wonder about going to church. I'll have to dress up, not that I have any church-going clothes.

The next morning Dr. Canter calls from the hospital to check in on me. I missed my last group therapy session.

"How is the job hunt going?" she asks.

"Fine. I applied for a job at the coffee house chain, 'Dark Boast,'" I say, very cleverly playing off the "Roast."

I can hear her stifle a laugh. "Jackson, I hope you didn't call it that at your interview."

"No, I'm more professional than that," I say rather irritated. "But I don't know if it's the right fit for me. Too much frantic busyness. I'd prefer working at the bookstore down the street."

She pauses for a moment. Collects her thoughts. "You can't keep hiding out from life, Jackson. Engage."

"Just jump into the deep end, huh?"

"Well, you did work at a lake once, if I recall," she laughs. A joke. I like it.

"That's funny, Doctor. I get it. Okay, but I still haven't heard back from them."

"You will, Jackson." I wonder if she has been talking to Steven, or God. "Are you making friends with your new housemates?"

"Yeah, but I'm still the odd man out."

"I understand how you would feel that way. You're unique, Jackson. That's why you like Pollock's paintings."

This makes me think of Jennifer again. I wonder if I should contact her. I get back on point. "You know my hands still shake, my stomach tingles, my mouth is constantly dry, and I have trouble pissing."

"That's all normal. I'll adjust the medication. How are you feeling mentally?"

"I get caught up in thought a lot, worrying about the future. Everything seems so vague."

"That's why you need to be in school and start working in the world. It will give you clarity about yourself, and your future will gradually come into focus."

I look out my window and watch seemingly content people, who are just living their lives, pass by on the street. They're holding down jobs and not freaking out, and I wonder what the hell is wrong with me, or why I can't accept that role for myself. Maybe it's hanging out with the misfits at the meetings. I tell Dr. Canter that

I'm tired of outpatient group therapy, and I ask her what's the point of all of it.

"It's part therapy and part socialization. You'll see." She pauses. "What writers do you like?" I tell her I just found *Tropic of Cancer* at the bookstore and that I couldn't stop reading it, and that Henry Miller seems to have found an acceptance and a transcendent life somehow.

"Maybe that's the real point of it all," Canter says. "I haven't read Miller, but some spiritually inclined writers have come to see the transcendence of the everyday world. You don't have to go to mountaintops, or surf in Costa Rica to find your meaning. It's right outside your window." I look back out the window, and I swear I see a light around everything. It must be the drugs. Or maybe it's God? I think about Steven. Maybe he's on to something.

I sit in one of the long, dreary meetings in the smoke-stained room in the basement of the hospital with weathered walls that have absorbed years of people's venting, purging and weeping. These walls have seen too many hard lives and tormented faces full of pain, regret, disappointment, failure, loss of love and hope, drug and alcohol addiction, physical and mental abuse. Wilting walls that have seen brave, scared, and sad faces in an endless flood of hurt and confusion wash through day after day, month after month, year after year leaving behind their psychic debris. A purgatory of pain. People smoking and drinking shitty coffee under the listless lights with their laments about life. *Life* is always waiting on the outside, lurking beyond the shatter-proof windows that hold in the pain and make reaching out to the world seem impossible.

"So, Jackson, what do you think?" asks the pre-pubescent-looking therapist. Much too perky for this early in the morning.

"I think there's a lot of pain in the world and a lot of sadness." I can feel everyone looking at me. My face flushes hot.

"How do you mean, Jackson?" the therapist asks.

"I mean, I hardly ever see anyone smiling."

"Do you ever smile, Jackson?" she asks me. I feel like I'm on the hot seat. Why did I open my big mouth? I calm myself and think about it for a second.

"Sometimes I smile at people on the street or on buses and BART, and they just look at me like I'm crazy, or think I want something from them.

"Well, I think you have a nice smile, Jackson. And I hope that you keep on smiling." She looks around the group. "Speaking of smiling. Did you know that studies have shown that when people smile their moods actually improve? And that when they frown, it decreases?" She looks around the room for smiles. Only me and an older woman, with turquoise jewelry and a flowing hippie shirt with flowers stitched on it, take the bait. This hippie woman gives a lukewarm smile, but my smile is big. I'm tired of being depressed. The third-grade therapist smiles back at me, her eyes widening behind her Owl-round glasses.

"It's along the lines of the Taoist saying by Lao Tzu. Does anyone know it?" Blank stares. "No? Okay, well it goes like this, 'Your thoughts become your words, your words become your actions, your actions become your habits, and your habits become your destiny.'" Her smile is wide, scanning the room for a spark of recognition, a hint of life. "Does anyone understand what I'm getting at?" No one's biting. Her spiel may seem a little Pollyanna, but it's a room full of life-hardened faces. Tough crowd. I raise my hand to bail her out.

"I think what you're getting at," I say, smiling. "Is that we have control over how we feel. Is that it?"

"Yes, Jackson. Exactly. And thank you." She proceeds undeterred, without skipping a beat, "Okay! I'll leave you with this saying, and then I'll let you go. Promise! Eleanor Roosevelt once said, 'No one can make you feel anyway that you don't want to!'" She looks around the room, nodding her head at the wisdom that she's just dropped on us. The hippie woman nods her head, and I smile, determined to give back a little of what she's giving us.

"Also!" she adds, as the group begins dispersing solemnly, one of the hard cases mumbling, *bullshit*, under his breath, "And don't forget to hug someone today . . . It'll make you feel better."

She trails off, looking a little defeated. I get up and give her a big hug. "Oh . . . Thank you, Jackson," she says, a little surprised, then looks up at me. "I think you're going to be okay. I have a good feeling about you."

I had decided to take BART (Bay Area Rapid Transit) to the group therapy session today, so that I could stay away from the halfway house a little longer. I've been feeling a little cooped up. I feel like I'm ready to spread my wings and fly out of this purgatory-like reality. I walk along the sidewalk from the hospital in a sort of trance, thinking about the quote from Lao Tzu as the sun peeks out from behind the fog, momentarily blinding me. I make my way to the station and try to track my thoughts. *No bad thoughts,* I tell myself as I see a train moving toward the station up ahead. I start running, and for some reason, running like my life depends on it. *You can do this asshole!* I yell to myself. Just as I make it to the station, the train is already getting ready to pull out. I jump the turnstile and hear the transit cop yelling at me as I make it through the doors just as they're closing. I'm panting, and my lungs are burning. I feel the adrenaline rush through my body like I could run a marathon. Suddenly, I see the reproachful looks of other passengers and realize that I'm smiling, then laughing. Maybe this is what Dr. Canter meant by jumping back into life.

26.

Sunday comes and I go to pick up Steven for church. I drive past row after row of small brick houses on manicured lawns on my way out into the suburbs. Steven's street is filled with a kind of desperate quiet. The trees are still. The air is still. All is frozen in this everywhere/nowhere suburbia. I can imagine the occupants with towels in their mouths screaming. Let's not disturb the neighbors.

His Ma answers the door. She looks old and fragile through the screen door. "Steven," she calls out meekly, "your friend is here." I look into the house at the dark interior. I smell mothballs and decay as a wave of sadness engulfs me, almost chokes my throat. It's too painful seeing where he lives, seeing how he lives. It makes his sadness all too real. I think about turning around and leaving just as he appears out of the dullness—large, ambling and smiling. He steps past his Ma. I look at him and wonder if he's going to tell me the meaning of life, as he had alluded to in the hospital weeks ago.

"We're goin' to church, Ma," he says, as he walks out the door.

"Okay," she says, "you boys have a nice day. Don't be out too late."

"I know, Ma! I won't be, Ma!"

"Jackson," Stevens says as we get in the car, "I think you're really going to like this service. You might even write about it in your book." He glances over at me. "You're still writing your book, aren't you?"

"Yes, of course. The words are flying off the page," I say, feeling guilty about lying to him. I wonder why, suddenly realizing that I miss writing, that I actually enjoyed it.

The Catholic church is just down the street. There are more cars in the parking lot than I expected. The air suddenly turns stale. I hate church services. I think back to the first time I went to church as a kid. All my friends were going, and I told my mom I wanted to go too. So, one day she picked me up from school and took me to the mall to get some "church clothes." I felt very important, like I was being fitted to be the next class president or something. She let me pick out whatever I wanted. She seemed proud of me, even though she didn't go to church much anymore. I got a pair of khaki pants, a light blue button-down shirt, a dark red tie with polo players on it, a pair of red socks and brown penny loafers. I was so excited for Sunday to come and be able to wear my new church outfit that I could hardly make it through the school week. When Sunday finally came, I put on my new clothes, combed my hair just right—part on the left side, bangs hanging down just a little, sides combed back over the ears— and I stepped out the door into the sunlight of the spirit.

But all I learned that day was what hypocrites most people who go to church are. I remember the immense whiteness of the interior and the starchy feeling of it all. Everyone's clothes were starched, smelled weird, and made that irritating whisking noise when they walked. Their hair was stiff, as were their handshakes, even their smiles felt forced. All the kids were bored out of their skulls and could hardly hold still. The adults seemed condescending to me, or patronizing, giving me dirty glances and whispering to others as I walked past them. I knew that they were judging me because my parents didn't come to church regularly, and therefore, I was an outcast. The service seemed to go on for an eternity, and I couldn't wait for it to be over so I could go home and take off my stupid clothes. Afterward I felt defeated and deflated, as if some essence had been sucked out of me, thinking that I didn't want to have anything to do with a place like that.

The service has already started, and Steven begins singing along to the memorized hymns as he looks for a place for us to sit. I mouth the words as we climb into a wooden pew in the back of the half-full, musty church.

The service goes on for what seems like forever. There's a lot of singing and back-and-forth repetition, "Lord, have mercy," "Christ have mercy," etc. We're in the back so I can still smell the incense but can hear a few people upfront choke on it. Steven knows the words to every song. He hands me a book, and I read aloud with the others, then close my eyes like I'm filled with the spirit. I open my eyes for a second. Steven nods approvingly. Finally, a sermon comes, then the blood of Christ and a wafer cookie. As everybody marches up for their wafer, I look at Steven.

"Need to go to confession before You can go to communion."

"Don't we all," I add. He smiles, despite himself.

Afterwards as we sit outside on a bench under a gray and pensive sky, Steven asks me, "What did you think about the service, Jackson?" His eyes show a flicker of life. Maybe the Holy Spirit has touched him.

"I liked the rituals, and that it's in English not Latin," I say. I look over my shoulder back at the church. "And the stained-glass windows, but my favorite part was drinking the blood of Christ. I feel like that helps a lot of people."

"That's exactly why you should become a Catholic, Jackson, and go to church. You need to let Jesus into your soul through communion." I actually consider this prospect. "We all need help, Jackson," he says.

"I don't know, Steven. Still seems like a stretch to me. Too much outward activity. I think I'd rather learn to meditate or something."

"The outward takes you inward, Jackson. We have to meet God halfway."

"Okay. Don't want to disappoint you, but I'm not sure yet that there's a God, Steven."

"Oh, that's not good, Jackson." He looks up at the sky. "I'll pray for you."

"Thanks, Steven. I appreciate that."

There is a long silence. The leaves blow by our bench. A little rain starts to fall.

"I don't know what I'm gonna do about my life, Jackson," he says, shaking his head.

"You'll be okay, Steven," I say, wanting it to be true but not sure that it will. He turns and smiles at me. His eyes are wet behind his thick, foggy glasses.

"Thanks. You're a good friend. Let's go see how Ahmad is doing." This is our Middle Eastern friend from the hospital, the one with the wild hair who once told me to never get married. Apparently, it didn't work out for him.

"You know where he lives?" I asked.

"Yeah, it's not far from here."

We drive slowly through the streets under the gently weeping sky as Steven tries to get his bearings. We take a couple of wrong turns. He swears but tells God he's sorry.

"I think this is it Jackson."

"This dump?" It looks like an empty building with a junk store on the bottom floor.

"This is the address he gave me, Jackson."

"Okay. Let's take a look."

We park on the abandoned street and step out. I peer through the dirty junk store windows at the piles and piles of old stuff.

Steven bangs on the door, calling out Ahmad's name as the falling rain starts to pick up.

"Ahmad! Ahmad!" No one answers. "I don't think anyone is home, Jackson," Steven says and looks devastated. I feel ashamed that I'm glad he's not home, if this is home, as I don't want to take on his sadness too. "Let's go Jackson," Steven finally says. "I gotta get home soon, or Ma will start to worry. I'm all she's got."

I nod my head. I know the feeling.

The day is turning darker, and we drive back to Steven's house in silence as he stares out the passenger's window at the empty wet streets. Kind of sums up the day for me.

When I pull into Steven's driveway, he looks over at me. "Think about giving God a chance, Jackson," he says solemnly.

"I will Steven. It's next on my list." He smiles.

As he gets out of the car, a well of sadness rises up in me and for some reason I know that it will be the last time I ever see Steven. He won't make it, and that makes me even sadder. I want to cry but I hold it back. I drive away and look back at him in the rearview mirror, a forlorn figure standing on the steps. Almost instinctively, I make the sign of the cross.

27.

The next day the phone rings waking me up. The house is empty. It's Dark Roast. I got the job. And for a brief moment I feel hopeful, actually ready to jump back into life.

I'm sent to a couple of days of training with a group of about ten other guys and girls from all over the city at a downtown building in an all-white boardroom that looks out over the bay. We go over company policy.

"Be polite at all times, no matter how your customers act or react. That's rule number one." I smile. Don't toss scalding-hot cups of coffee at any dickheads. I got it.

There's a dress code: Khakis pants and skirts and black shoes to go with our black shirts and blue aprons. We each get a $50 clothing voucher for one of the GAP stores.

Then they tell us about all the different kinds of coffee from all over the world: Guatemalan. Columbian. Ethiopian. They pass bags of different kinds of beans around the room so that we can sniff them. We take sips of the coffees from tiny Dixie cups. It reminds me of med-time in the hospital. I like the Ethiopian the best. It has an earthy smell. I'm wired on coffee today. My hands shake a bit. I try to steady them. No more coffee for me.

Then they show us how to make the coffee in their gleaming silver dispensers that look like they could transport your soul back in time, or to wherever they grow this stuff. They show us how to steam milk, make espressos, cappuccinos and lattes. While this takes up a whole morning, it doesn't seem that difficult. I definitely won't fall asleep. I can do this job and become a gainfully and respectfully employed member of society. I can see my Mom smiling, and I make a note to call and tell her.

On the final day we take turns working a makeshift counter, taking orders for coffee from our fellow workers in the Dark Roast dialect, dispensing them and smiling. I've had too much coffee again. I'm jittery as I hand off my first cup of coffee. I tell the cute girl I like the way her hair shines. I smile awkwardly - that didn't come out right; she smiles back, but the instructor shakes his head. My small-talk radar is warped. Already labelled a misfit.

We all collect our new clothes and head out. A few of the others head for a local restaurant/bar. I decline. The shiny haired girl looks disappointed, which makes me smile. But the last thing I need to do is have a couple of drinks and tell everyone how I just got out of the mental hospital, and that I'm living in a halfway house.

The next morning, I head for work at 5:00 am, my shift starts at 5:30. I'm glad all the guys are still asleep. Hate for them to see me in my Dark Roast outfit. Luckily, I should get back before they return from their jobs. I drive there and start work. My hands are shaking as I'm setting out the pastries. People are already lined up outside in the dark, knocking on the glass doors to get in. I'm sweating. It must be the medication. We're not even open yet. It's 5:30 in the damn morning! The shiny hair girl with the soft eyes asks me if I'm okay.

"Yeah. Just a little nervous."

"Don't worry, you'll get the swing of it. That smile of yours will cover up a lot of mistakes." Nice.

I force a smile. It seems to be my best assett. *I can do this . . . It's not rocket science.* I stare straight ahead at the pastries, concentrating and trying to make my hands stop shaking. I may have to go off the meds to do this job. I picture myself crying over the pastries, then throwing them up in the air. Sweat trickles down the back of my neck. *I can do this*, I keep telling myself. The line of people is getting longer and longer out there in the darkness. They need their morning caffeine fix. I can't get my hands to stop shaking. What in the hell is wrong with me? My mouth is dry. It's gotta be the meds. I think of the oranges that Koran used to give me in the hospital, and I wonder if everyone sees me as crazy as I frantically try to arrange the stupid fucking pastries in the display bin and then suddenly the doors open. People begin to rush in like we're a crack house that's been out of the white rocks for a month. My boss comes out of nowhere and seemingly more wired than I am. He animatedly tells me that we are one of the busiest coffee shops in the country, then puts me on the register and says, "You'll be fine!"

I'm anything but fine as the people blurt out their orders in the made-up Dark Roast coffee language, and I can't understand what the hell they're saying! I have to keep looking back at the menu on the wall to figure out the orders, as they shake their arms and heads and point animatedly behind me. I feel like I'm either stupid or they're crazy, as I write chicken scratch on endless cup after cup. All my verbal responses are stuck in my desert-dry throat. I can't seem to focus or ring up the register, and talk at the same time. I need oranges. I peer into an endless sea of scowls attached to black and gray business suits and sour-faced housewives with demanding eyes. My hands shake like I've got dementia, and my mouth is a dustbowl. I try to act normal. But I'm not. One of the female customers asks me if I'm okay. This shocks me. Someone cares.

"My first day."

A guy in line says, "It shows." He must be one of the dickheads they mentioned in training.

I smile.

The woman glares back at him. She turns to me. "Do it at your own pace, son. Soon the repetition will take over, and it'll be smoother."

"Thanks, Mom." She smiles.

This little bit of kindness helps. My hands stop shaking as much, and I get through the morning without incident before I'm relieved from the register and the pagan coffee hoards.

I drive home from work shell-shocked trying to figure out how I'm going to make it through another day on this job. I'm tempted to stop off at the corner bar and down a few cold ones, but it's only late afternoon. And I want to get back home and change before the guys see me in these duds.

At home I change, and step out to the back porch. Normally, after a shock-and-awe experience like this first day at work, I'd hear Aaron in my head telling me to tell them to piss off. But I know I've got to stick with it. *Keep a positive attitude, dude. Things will get better.*

The next day goes better. The manager keeps me off the register on the first shift and has me pouring coffee. "Seems like a better fit for you. The register can be a bitch at first."

No kidding.

I work the register on the afternoon shift, and I'm starting to get the hang of it. Then, I turn back to my next customer. It's Jennifer. She flashes me a big beautiful smile and for a moment I'm frozen. She's like a beaming oasis in a sea of bleak, arid faces. I feel my heart race. Out of her hospital scrubs, with her brown hair down and lipstick on, she prettier than I remember, striking. Luckily, she's the only one in line.

"Jennifer!" I say, trying not to give away too much of my excitement.

"Jackson! It's good to see you," she says smiling. "You look like you're doing great!"

"I'm doing *okay*. What are you doing here? I mean, do you live in the neighborhood?"

"Well . . ." She looks around the coffee shop, as though we could be under surveillance. "Can you keep a secret?"

"I probably can't remember it anyway. My head's filled with coffee nonsense. But I'll do my best." I too look around the coffee shop. "I think the coast is clear." She laughs. *Good* one. I'm getting back into the swing of things.

"Dr. Canter may have told me you were working here . . . and it's officially against HIPA regulations to have contact with a patient within six months of their discharge. So, I'm not really here."

"I promise not to call HIPA."

She laughs. "Okay. Funny Jackson." She pauses. "Can you take a break and sit down for a minute?"

She looks back at the mostly empty black chairs scattered around the shiny wooden tables. It's the mid-afternoon lull, I'm told.

"Sure, let me just get someone to take the register. Do you want a coffee?"

"I'll take a small latte."

I look at the manager sitting at a table doing paperwork. He's been watching us. I smile. He nods his head.

I turn to the shiny hair girl, who is staring at Jennifer walking away.

"Can you watch the register for a minute?" I ask her, as I start to make her latte.

She shrugs her shoulders and smirks. "Sure. Is that one of your teachers?" I laugh. I like her attitude.

I sit down next to Jennifer and slide the latte over to her.

"Thank you," she says. Conversation from a nearby table and the sound of hissing espresso machines give us a bit of privacy.

"So, what's up?" I ask.

"Well, you know I wanted to use the art therapy paintings your group did in an art show that I was putting together?"

"I remember. And if I remember correctly, you thought mine was the best." She laughs.

"I did and I do," she says. "Actually, yours is really good . . . And I'm highlighting it. Tomorrow night is the opening of the show, and I wanted to see if you'd accompany me there?"

I lean back and look at her in disbelief. "Really," she adds, probably relishing the effect this invite has on me.

"Of course, I'd love to."

"Great!" she says, briefly putting her hand on mine. She keeps talking, but I'm only half- listening, feeling a little fuzzy, a little dizzy. "The show is at the University of Berkeley where I go to school."

"I won't have to give a talk or anything?" I ask, starting to feel a bit overwhelmed.

"No, Jackson. You can trust me. I'll watch your back."

"Okay . . ."

"Then, it's decided. I'll pick you up at your house at 6 o'clock and take you to this great second-hand store in Berkley that has amazing avant-garde men's clothing. We want you to look the part."

I start to protest, but Jennifer squeezes my hand. "Okay. But I'm not a real artist."

"No. You're who you are, and I want the world to see what I see in you."

I almost blush. "Avant-garde?" She laughs. "Okay." I say

tentatively. My hands start to slightly shake. She holds them still.

"Good. Write down your address and I'll see you at six,

tomorrow."

28.

The next day I'm sitting by the window, looking out at the street, a

nervous, anticipatory energy consuming me. It doesn't help that all

of the guys have just come home from work.

"You look like a puppy, waiting for its owner to come home

to let it go out to pee," Brock says, and the other guys laugh as they

raid the refrigerator. Just then, Jennifer's silver BMW convertible

pulls into the driveway. The sun reflects off of her big white

sunglasses.

Brock walks through the living room as I get up. "Is she here

to pick you up?" he asks, obviously jealous. All the other guys come

piling over the window to see what's going on.

"She's taking me to an art opening."

"What?" he says, looking me up and down, then laughs. "Dressed like that?" He looks out at Jennifer. She looks amazing, like a movie star in a black cocktail dress. The guys are pushing each other out of the way to get a better look at her.

"Holy shit!" Jason, my roommate says, his eyes widening. "She's hot as hell!" Jennifer taps the horn smiling, waving for me to come on. She sees the stir that she's causing and is relishing it. "Son of bitch, Jackson. You've got a hot, rich girlfriend!"

"Good for you, Bro," the large Samoan guy says flatly. Jennifer taps the horn again.

I scamper down the steps, open up the passenger's side door, and slide onto the tan leather seat. Jennifer smiles, puts her hand on my knee as though sensing my tension.

"This is going to be fun, Jackson." She winks at me. Jennifer backs out of the driveway, then puts the car in drive and waves to the guys in the window as she hits the gas and speeds off.

The sun is shining down on me as the wind whips through my hair, the car stereo blasting the *Rolling Stones, Can't Get No Satisfaction.* If only Bill could see me now. I feel as though I'm watching the final scene of a movie where the guy drives off into the sunset with the pretty girl. I feel a rush of energy surge through me and realize

how glad I am alive to experience this moment.

Jennifer looks over at me, as though reading my mind. "Nice

to be out of the hospital, huh?" she yells over the stereo and the

wind.

I smile at her. "Let's have some fun."

"It's your night!" She smiles back. "We're going to get you

some trendy clothes, Mr. Jackson Smith, artist!" she adds and steps

on the gas.

As we get nearer to the University of Berkeley campus,

students start appearing like ants out of a massive mound. They walk

in hordes, some with backpacks looking deadly serious, others

talking and laughing, a group throwing a football as they walk. The

sun is setting, and neon lights of the coffee shops, restaurants, and

stores lining the street blink on.

"This is the main drag," Jennifer says, turning down the

stereo. I nod, vaguely remembering it from a childhood expedition

here with my grandmother. The air smells like a mix of incense,

cooking food and pine trees. It feels insular and safe, full of promise.

Worlds away from the seemingly forgotten edge where I live with my dropout roommates. Jennifer pulls down an alleyway, makes a sharp right down another alley, pulling into a parking spot next to a dumpster behind a one-story brick building covered in graffiti.

"This is the place," Jennifer says as we climb out of the car.

We walk toward the building and I open the back door for her. "You know, you don't have to do this, Jennifer. You're a college student. Money must be tight."

"Not really. And I can afford to splurge on my new friend." *She* looks at me. "Relax and just step into it, Big Guy."

Punk music is being pumped through the store from a CD player next to the cashier. Different genres of band posters cover the walls from *Led Zeppelin* to *Nirvana*, the *Sex Pistols* to *Jimmy Hendrix* and so on. Chandeliers hang throughout the space, illuminating the overflowing racks and racks of clothes and shoes. Pierced and tattooed employees with mohawks or dyed hair watch over it all. Jennifer looks at me. "You really don't know why I'm doing this for you?" I shake my head, No. "You've got a good heart, Jackson. I saw the way you reached out to the others in the hospital. Most people would've looked down on them. The Buddhist call it 'Loving Kindness.'" She smiles. "So, call this good karma."

I feel like such a baby as my eyes tear up. She wipes her hands across my face, puts her hands on the back of my neck, then leans in to kiss me. A feeling of white, hot bliss shoots through me as everything goes black and silent for a split second. Then the music kicks back in and the world continues to spin. *Oh shit, I'm in love.* I think. And if this is what Dr. Canter meant by life 'returning in kind', then I'm *in*.

"Jackson," Jennifer says, and I open my eyes. "You could be going to school here with me, studying literature, or creative writing. I know you were working on a book in the hospital."

"It was more journaling than anything."

"Well, either way you should think about it. If you do well at community college, establish residency, you could do it."

"I thought you were graduating this year."

"I am, but I'm working towards becoming a psychiatrist. Got a lot of years left before I leave here."

"I'll think about it," I say tentatively. Don't want to get ahead of myself, as things are already *swirling*.

She takes my hand, scans the store, then says, "Okay. Let's find you something to wear. But we've got to hurry. I need to be at the exhibition by seven and it's already a little after six. You go and find some shoes and I'll get a suit for you! What size are you?"

"Large, I guess." I haven't worn a suit in years.

She looks me over. "You're probably a 42," she says, shooing me away.

I scan the racks of shoes. All I can find in my size is a pair of faded black cowboy boots.

I take them over to Jennifer who is tearing through a rack of button-down shirts with her left hand as she holds a black suit with a set of red roses embroidered on each lapel.

"Perfect! Here. Hold this." She hands me the suit as she pulls out a shirt.

"This is a vintage Western suit," she says. "I told you they have good finds here. Quick, follow me." She says as we weave our way through the store to where we find an empty dressing room. Jennifer hands me the shirt. I step in and close the curtain behind me.

"Hurry, hurry, hurry," she says, as I start ripping off my clothes and putting on the new ones. She peeks her head around the corner, catching me in my underwear. "Mmmm," she says, smiling at me and biting her lower lip. "Hurry, hurry."

"I'm trying!" She slides the curtain closed and I throw on the clothes.

"Well! How do they fit? Do I need to grab something else?"

"Hold on. I'm just putting the shoes on." I try them on. I'm worried that I'm going to look like I'm wearing a costume. But everything feels alright, and when I look in the mirror, I like what I see.

"Come on!" Jennifer says anxiously. "Show me how it looks." I step out of the dressing room. She steps back, taking it in, then steps up to me grabbing the lapels of my jacket, unbuttons one of the buttons on the dress shirt, leans in and kisses me. "You look amazing *cowboy*, like a proper avant-garde artist. Now grab your clothes and just wear this out." She pulls off the tags off as we walk to the register.

As we drive the darkened streets, lit by gas lamps and the glow of stores, I think for a moment what my life could be like here, dating Jennifer, getting a small place of my own, studying literature, making friends and getting a job at a coffee shop/bookstore.

"What are you thinking about Jackson?" Jennifer asks, as we cruise through the streets.

"Coffee and the capitalistic money machine," I say, laughing.

"Hmm," she says looking over at me. "Heavy." I look down at the suit, the car I'm in, and wonder where Jennifer's money comes from. For the first time this evening I feel uncomfortable, like an outsider looking in. Again, she reads me like I'm an open book. "Don't worry, Jackson, it's going to be fun. You'll fit in. I promise."

"Okay," I say, but have to wonder if I'm just a pity case she's parading around like a novelty.

29.

On the edge of campus, just past seven, we pull up to a modern white, two-story building made up mainly of glass framed by concrete and steel, with angled lines and sharp corners, nestled in amongst massive old growth trees. Lights from inside the building illuminate the well-dressed people inside sipping drinks and mingling, as waiters walk around carrying trays of long-stem flutes of champagne. I'm amazed. This is an actual museum art show, not a pet school project.

"What's going on here, Jennifer?"

"Come on," Jennifer says. "Let's go in. You'll see!" She takes my arm as we step up to the sidewalk. "And remember," she says, glancing at me as we stride up the walkway, "no one is to know that you're one of the artists on display. I could get in trouble."

"Got it," I say, as we approach a stainless-steel placard that reads, *Berkley Center for the Arts*, Made possible by the Knowland Family Trust. I pull open one of the large glass doors for Jennifer, as I bow and wave her in. "Madam," I say with a big smile.

She pulls on the lapel of suit. "Behave," Jennifer says and winks at me. I put my arm around her waist and kiss her on the cheek as we step into a small reception area. There, two young women stand wearing a white cocktail dresses and holding the guest list. Each of them with blonde hair pulled back into ponytails. It's unnerving and a little intimidating. They each look at me with quizzical smiles. I feel like I'm on display. They turn their attention to Jennifer.

"Hi, Jennifer!" they say chirping in unison, then glance at me as though looking for an explanation—guardians of the threshold.

"This is my artist friend, Jason," she says. "His parents and mine are friends, and he just moved out here to go to school."

"Oh, cool," they say again in unison. I wonder if they're robots.

"So, you're going to school here at Cal?" the taller blonde asks.

"No, actually, I'm going to school at Oakland Community College." The girl looks confused.

Jennifer jumps in. "He's transferring to Cal next semester." She smiles back at the girls who look unimpressed, almost sour, as Jennifer pulls my arm, guiding me into the gallery. "I'll catch up with you later," she tells the girls. We walk on, as she takes two flutes of champagne from one of the two waiters posted patiently just inside the gallery space.

"From now on," Jennifer tells me, handing me a glass of champagne, "if people ask, tell them that you go to Cal."

"Why?" I ask. "I don't."

She looks at me, as though trying to choose her words carefully. "In this world, you are what you pretend to be," she says, staring at me intently. "And you are an artist, Jackson. So, act the part."

"Did you learn that in one of your psychology classes here at Berkeley?" I ask, a little defensively.

"No, actually, it's something that my father told me," she says gravely.

"What's wrong with just being me?"

"Nothing," Jennifer says, touching the rose above my heart. "Nothing at all. And that's what I want you to see, that there's a bigger world out there for you than what you've seen." She raises her glass. "Cheers, to your first art opening and the new you!" she says, and we clink glasses. The champagne tastes amazing. "Now I've got to go and say hi to some people. You explore the exhibit, and don't drink too many of these! I'll catch up with you in a bit. And don't forget that you're Jason tonight." She winks at me, raises her champagne flute in the air and disappears into the crowd. Immediately I hear people saying her name, "Jennifer! Jennifer! So good to see you! This show is *amazing*!"

I down my champagne to quell whatever unease I'm feeling and go looking for another glass. The crowd is dense. There are a lot more people than I expected. Maybe that's why I'm so nervous. Many of them look affluent and older. Then there's the younger, eclectic crowd sprinkled about in their *avant-garde*, eye-catching, yet fashion-conscious outfits. The whole place smells of expensive cologne and money. The champagne flutes and hors d'oeuvre are too hard to get through the crowd, so I make my way to the second floor, via the sweeping concrete staircase and glass railing that cuts through the space diagonally.

The second floor is less crowded, and I feel like I can breathe. I grab another glass of champagne from one of the waiters to help quiet the noise from the chaotic symphony of conversations and hopefully convince the butterflies in my stomach to stop moving. I take a long sip and notice a handful of seemingly misplaced guests wearing outfits that don't look fashionable or trendy or from money, but are instead, tired and worn, and even a disheveled couple. The artists, no doubt. I can see people watching them as the two girls at the front doors look up at me. I down the rest of my champagne and grab another glass. I feel the buzz and then realize that this is what Dr. Canter called self-medicating. I decide to take it easy, not sure how too much alcohol will mix with my medications, but it might be too late.

"Are you one of the artists?" someone to my left asks, as I stare down at the crowd of people and the amazing paintings trying to figure out this scene. A small man with gray hair, black round glasses, and a pink paisley handkerchief around his neck is standing next to me. "Quite an odd scene. Isn't it?" His voice is somewhere between annoying and effeminate. I nod my head, taking another sip of my champagne. "So, you are one of the artists."

"No. I'm not. I'm just here with a friend."

"Oh, I thought for sure you were an artist with that wonderful cowboy outfit you're wearing. You didn't come here on a horse, by chance, did you?"

"Actually, I think my friend's BMW has around 320 horses pulling it."

"Oh, wonderful come back. A smart lad."

I smile. Don't be so defensive. "I try."

"So, who is your friend then? If you don't mind me asking. One of the artists?" he asks, saying "artist" with amusement or derision. My face feels flushed. I feel out of my element with such a tool.

"No. I'm here with my friend, Jennifer. She put this show together."

"Oh, Jennifer," he says, looking me up and down, with an entirely different attitude. "Well, good for you, young man. Your ship has come in. It's quite impressive what she's done."

"Yes, the untrained artists angle is pretty cool, I guess."

"Well, no, it's not so much that . . ." he says, eyeing me somewhat condescendingly, "What's impressive is that she got her parents and the Knowland Family Trust to show their private collection alongside her pet 'project.'"

"What pet project?"

"Well, her gathering and nurturing the untrained misfits, I mean, untrained 'artists' who use art as emotional healing, or therapy or *whatever* . . . as I'm sure you know." He says, looking at me, knowing that I *don't* know. "Artists that she finds throughout the city, whose works she thinks are somehow reflective of all these famous artists' pieces. It's quite interesting, although the untrained artists' works she's gathered don't quite compare to the *real* things. I'm not saying of course that brilliance can't spring, untrained from the gutter or the streets, I mean, there's the Puerto Rican Basquiat.

But, it's a bit like hoping that a Mona Lisa will spring from a pile of horse maneur!" At this he lifts his wine glass. "Well, Cheers," he says.

"I'm sure this isn't news to you, but you're a real horse's ass," I say, surprised that words jumped from my mouth before I could choke them down. "Cheers," I mimic and down the rest of my glass as he back-peddles away. Probably afraid I'll knock him over the railing.

I look around the room feeling hot, a little dizzy, searching for a Jackson Pollock painting. I head downstairs, scanning the room from the concrete staircase as I descend. I see it, over the heads of the crowd, tucked away in the far back corner. I'm sweating and my mouth is dry as I make my way through the people to the Pollock.

It stops me in my tracks, and I stand and stare at it, transfixed by the sheer chaos of its mesmerizing beauty. I think back to the hospital that seems worlds and worlds away now, to the day that Koran and me and Greg and Jane made our chaotic paintings while Bill played his classic rock tunes. I look for *our* paintings, but there's only mine next to it. Mine from that day, matted and framed aside the Pollock, the name Jackson Smith engraved on a bronze placard under it. Jesus. And I hear a man standing next to me say, "Pollock may have been crazy, but at least he had talent, this poor person displayed next to him just got the crazy portion of the equation." I feel my heart sink. There's a dull buzzing in my ears. I look around the room that's slowly starting to spin. I feel like I may be sick. I see the red, neon-lit exit sign and begin pushing through the crowd, knocking a drink out of a woman's hand by accident, the glass shattering on the floor in my wake.

As I make it to the doors, I hear one of the blonde gatekeepers of the gallery say, "What's going on? Are you sick?" I don't have a suitable reply. I just need fresh air.

Outside on the sidewalk, I look up at the stars in the sky, which helps to orient me, and things have stopped spinning. I look around at my surroundings, to further get my bearings. I see Jennifer inside talking to an older man. He's speaking to her angrily, as a father to a daughter who's in trouble. He's pointing in my direction. She turns away from him and walks toward the exit.

"Jackson!" she yells, coming down the walkway towards me. "Are you alright? What happened in there? My father said you insulted one of his friends and that you broke a glass and stormed out. You're making a scene . . ."

I cut her off. "You've made this scene!" I shake my head. I don't have the words to express my anger. Finally, I blurt out, "You used me, Jennifer."

"What are you talking about? Are you drunk?"

"Maybe a little. Yes . . ." But that's not the point. "The point is that you used me. You used all of the street artists in there, if there's actually any artists amongst the hoity-toity."

"How? What are you talking about? I'm not following you, Jackson."

"As props, Jennifer. You used us as props to turn the spotlight on you. For all your supposed good intentions, your wanting to become a psychiatrist, it's just cultural voyeurism . . . You'll end up like the rest of those pretentious assholes in there."

"Jesus, Jackson," she says contritely, looking down. "That's . . . I'm sorry if you feel used, and I'm sorry that I hurt you. I really feel you and the other 'street' artists have promise, that the raw expression of your angst, despite a lack of artistic training, is just as legitimate. That's the whole point of the display. Art is 90% expression. Anybody can get training."

I feel a lump in my throat, and I feel like a bit of an asshole. She puts her hand on my arm, trying to calm me down. "And I know the 'asshole' you put down. Come back in with me, and I'll reem him myself."

"What about your father."

"Screw him." Jennifer looks very determined. "Go wait in the car. Let me say my goodbyes. Thirty minutes tops." She stares into my eyes. "Then we're leaving. Because if there's somebody I really want to screw, it's you, Jackson. Can you handle that?"

I take a big gulp. I'm speechless. She steps over, pulls my head to her, and kisses me long and hard. She turns, walks back to the showing. I look up and see her father staring at us and shaking his head. "Screw you," I say and walk back to her car.

30.

Diffused sunlight shines through the wood shutters into the silent white room, and I slowly start to wake up. My head aches and I wonder if I'm in the hospital again. Or, maybe I've gone too far this time and I'm in the ER. But the all-too-familiar sense of underlying dread suddenly turns to comfort as I feel the warmth of a silky thigh against mine. I look over to make sure that I'm not dreaming and see Jennifer sleeping soundly, her brown hair spread across the silver silk of her pillow. I look up at the ceiling, painted to look like a cloudy sky, trying to remember all that happened last night. I slip out of bed quietly and begin searching for my clothes. As I sit on the velvety green footstool at the end of the bed putting on my cowboy clothes, I look around the loft. Everything is tidy and orderly. Everything from the furniture to the spice rack in the kitchen has its reason and its place. I'm the only thing that feels foreign. I pull on the black boots and look over at Jennifer, peacefully sleeping, her arms and legs exposed. I stand up and step to her side of her bed, gently pulling the sheets up to cover her, run my hand across her hair, then lean in and kiss her on the cheek.

On the kitchen counter, I find a piece of scratch paper and a pen. After writing her a note saying that I'll talk to her later, I slip out the door before she wakes.

As I wait for the elevator, I stare out the window at the other high-rise buildings of downtown San Francisco. It's foggy and gray out, and I can't see across the bay toward Berkeley.

As I ride the elevator down to the parking garage, I see flashbacks from last night of me and Jennifer driving across the Bay Bridge with the top down, the music turned up loud, her singing along enthusiastically to, Prince's *Purple Rain*. Me laughing at how surreal life can be.

"To your first art show!" she yelled, looking over at me, smiling, as the lights of San Francisco twinkled ahead of us through the fog.

My head aches as I step out of the glass elevator foyer into the parking garage. The BMW is parked near the elevators in a reserved spot. The top is still down, like I was hoping. I take my old clothes out of the bag and change back into them right next to the car. Nobody is around. I fold up my cowboy suit and leave it in the back with the black boots.

I take the elevator back up to the lobby with its shiny marble floors, its floor-to-ceiling windows, and its steel columns. A stern-looking security guard is giving me the stink eye.

"Can you tell Jennifer Knowland that the top of her car is still down?" I say to him, and his frown turns into a smile—any reason to talk with the beautiful Jennifer. He nods his head as I walk out. *Lucky guy*, I can see him thinking.

Outside I look up at the high rise where Jennifer lives. It's cloudy, cool, and gray out. Looks like it may have rained a little during the night. A few cars pass by slowly, making that slightly squishing sound of tires passing on wet asphalt. I look around the clean streets feeling a little disoriented, but also feeling like a psychic weight has been lifted from me, like something inside of me has shifted. The long downward slide is over, and I can move on, I hope.

As I start to walk down the street, I think about how charmed Jennifer's life is, wondering if I could fit into her world. I look down at my coffee-stained clothing and worn-leather shoes. *Probably not.* I think back to all the patients in the mental ward who said how fortunate I am. I look around the downtown area at some of the homeless, huddled in corners for warmth, waiting to panhandle the locals. It's all relative, I guess. I know I just want to be comfortable with who I am.

I'm a little cold and pick up the pace, looking for the nearest bus stop. I need to get to the hospital this morning for my last group. By contrast the streets start to come alive with the frantic busyness of self-important men in suits, carrying briefcases. Titans of capitalism and industry, pour out of the high-rise apartment buildings, all of them looking as dull and as gray as the streets they're walking. I picture Jennifer's dad pointing at me last night from the gallery window, as though I were a stray dog that had just taken a crap on his lawn. He probably owns the building that Jennifer lives in. And I realize that if I were to stay with Jennifer and go to Berkeley, (not that this is a real possibility) her dad would probably end up owning me, that I'd probably become one of these sour-faced Suits endlessly trying to stack up the most cheese cubes. I smile and think about the book, *Who Moved My Cheese*.

I find a bus stop and the bus comes shortly. As I sit quietly watching the other passengers in the morning stillness, I wonder where they're all going. The sun starts to part the fog. I can feel its warmth on my face as the slow rolling rhythm of the bus nearly puts me to sleep, and my mind starts to reel like a movie projector playing through the scenes from last night. I can see Jennifer coming back out of the gallery, smiling at me, the light from inside illuminating her from behind, like an angel's halo . . . As she drives, I put my hand on her thigh, the streetlights and shop lights streaking by in green, yellow, blue and white . . . The moon is high, full, and bright . . . And she takes my hand as we step into the darkness of her place . . . Then we're kissing and stumbling through the maze of furniture as we're trying to take our shoes off, making our way to her bed in the far corner of the large open space . . . Then her hands are in my hair, her breath is warm on my neck, and her kisses wet as I slip off her dress.

Leaning back on the bed and pulling me onto it with her.

"Be gentle," I whisper. Half in jest.

She laughs and kisses me.

In her arms, time seemed to stand still. I felt myself come to life. Jennifer, the goddess who brought me back from the dead.

I come back from this reel just before my stop, get off, and walk several blocks to the hospital. I'm feeling detached from the motions that I'm going through, feeling like I've been hit by a tsunami. Or maybe Steven's God?

In the basement room of the hospital where the group meets, I get a cup of strong coffee and take a seat in the back, hoping to disappear into the wall, my head still aching a little from last night's champagne. And silently I make a vow, like I do with every hangover, to never drink again. People begin to slowly filter inside, some stopping and chatting by the coffee table, ranging in ages from eighteen to seventy.

We have a motivational speaker today. He looks like a very nice man in his early sixties, with a lined and weathered face, neatly buzzed white hair and piercing blue eyes. He says he used to be crazy and broken and hopeless once, like most of us, and everyone laughs.

"I used to have it *all* too!" he says, his eyes lighting up, his arms reaching out as though to hug the whole world. "I had a big house, great car, nice clothes, silk suits, and a very pretty wife . . . Hell, I even had a boat. I used to sail around the Bay. Can you believe that?" Everyone shakes their heads, *No.* But I believe him, the way his eyes shine, remembering those things. "But you know what?" he asks the room. Most everyone shakes their head again, *No.* "I wasn't happy. It was never enough. All the money, and all those material things. There was always something more I needed to fill the empty hole inside of me. *Nothing*, no amount of money, no amount of finery, no amount of drugs or alcohol, or women, or whatever your thing is, will fill it." He trails off, looking around the room for dramatic effect. Everyone nods, like they have a *thing*. Alcohol is my thing. "And you know what?" he asks, knowing that he's got the whole room's attention. Everyone in the room shakes their heads, *No*. "When it all came crashing down, I had no idea who I really was." He shakes his head, looking down at the floor. "And," he says, looking back up, "I realized that I didn't like my job. I realized that I didn't like the person I had become. I didn't like the person I was married to. My kids sure as hell didn't like me, and I had no real friends." There's a long silence as he scans the room, as though waiting for a reaction.

"So, what do you do now?" a woman in her mid-thirties, with dark circles under her eyes, wearing a red hoodie, with her hair pulled up in a ponytail asks. Her face has a beaten look.

"Well, that's a good question," he says, smiling at her. "First, I had to ditch the drugs and the alcohol. Then, I did a lot of soul searching . . ." He looks around the room, his eyes smiling like he's about to let us in on a big secret. I begin thinking it's probably some version of Steven's "the Meaning of Life" shit.

"Then I did a lot of research into what makes people happy or what makes them *satisfied* with their lives." He looks at us intently, to make sure we're still paying attention, and I realize I'm glad I came to this group, like maybe it's the Universe talking to me, and that this guy is just a medium? "And, you know what I found?"

"No . . ." the room says in unison.

"What I found out, was that what you have to do, is to pursue something that you're truly passionate about!" He points up to the ceiling to help make his point. "And in pursuing that, you will find purpose and meaning in your life."

"So, what do you do, then?" the woman in the red hoodie asks again, smiling a little sheepishly, like she's picturing back to childhood and remembering something that she once loved.

"Well, I do this," he says and looks around the room. "I do motivational speaking, and I write self-help books, and I counsel people, people like you. I don't make a lot of money, just enough to pay the bills and get by. But I'm content. I feel like my life has purpose and meaning, and my children speak to me now, even ask

me for advice sometimes," he smiled, "and I feel good about
myself."

My grandparents know the guy who wrote, *Chicken Soup for
the Soul*, because my grandpa gave his wife piano lessons. They
became good friends, because grandpa Smith is a really interesting
and nice man, who tells great stories and loves to laugh. Anyway, he
gave me the book, and I thought it was a little hokey, honestly, and I
think it's probably like the books this guy writes. But I'm also
starting to realize that a lot of things that I've thought were hokey
are probably right on.

I feel terrible that I haven't been to visit my grandparents and
I make another silent vow to myself that I'll go and see them soon.

On the bus ride back to Oakland, the sky is clear and blue as
we cross the Bay Bridge. I look back toward San Francisco and the
Golden Gate bridge in the distance and think about the day I stood
by the railing with the wind gusting, feeling like I wanted to jump
and end it all. And I realize that I don't recognize that person
anymore. It's another version of me that I've shed forever, a version
of me that had no clue what he wanted to do with his life. I think
about what the speaker said in the group this morning, and I know I

have to make a decision, choose a direction. I think about Jennifer and going to Berkeley and know that's not for me. Writing is the only thing that I feel gives me any kind of purpose, any meaning. A place to start. But first, I have to get out of the halfway house where I'm living. I think about my future as the bus hums along making its way into Oakland.

When I arrive home, Jason is passed out on the couch with. The television is on MTV, blasting a video by Oasis, "Wonderwall." I don't know what *you're my wonderwall* means, as the lead singer sings, but I get the impression that it's something only a woman can be, and it's something that a man needs. Maybe it's what Jennifer gave me last night or showed its possibilities? Maybe something that connects you to the rest of the world? I'm not sure, but I like the sound of it.

When I see the note taped to my bedroom door, I know that I'm in trouble. But I don't really care. I unfold the note as I open my bedroom door. *We need to talk. Brock.* Is all it reads. I crumple it up and throw it in the trash can on the floor under the splintery old beat-up desk. My roommate is gone, and I close the blinds, take off my clothes and climb into bed. I need to sleep it off before I confront

Brock and his idiocy.

31.

It's late afternoon when Brock pounds on my door, then sticks his

big head inside the room and shouts, "Get up, Jackson. We need to

talk."

"Yeah, I got your note."

"Come on. Get your clothes on." I rub my eyes, sit up in bed.

I don't like confrontations, especially with dickheads. I take a deep

breath and think of what my options are. I find my black Champion

sweat suit. Put it on and walk out into the living room where Brock

and Trevor are sitting next to each other on the edge of the couch.

"Are you two a couple now?" I ask, thinking they look like

my parents waiting to talk to me after a night out drinking. Neither

of them thinks it's very funny. *Bad start,* I say to myself.

"Ha. Ha," Trevor says, annoyed.

"Sit down," Brock adds sternly.

"Am I grounded?" I ask, sitting down, not liking this parent

routine. I'm just going to let caution fly to the wind; let the chips fall where they may. I have a strange *faith* today that things are going to be okay.

"Okay, here's the deal," Brock says. "You didn't have an overnight pass, and you didn't come in last night. So, technically, we can kick you out." I wonder if they're bluffing, but he's holding what looks like a rule book. I didn't even read the house rules, and I had to work some of our house meeting nights.

Trevor looks at me. "But we're not going to do that. Instead, we're going to fine you, as a warning: $150."

I look at them both like they're crazy. "That's in the rule book?" I ask, figuring that they're shaking me down.

"No. It isn't," Brock says, almost leering at me. "And you don't have to pay it, and we kick you out, but you forfeit your $300 deposit, which is what you'll need to get into another house. So, it's your decision." Time stands still for a moment as my mind runs through all my options. I see a kid across the street riding his red big wheel, his mom following behind him. And I remember when I was young and innocent, and now I'm being blackmailed by two idiotic thugs, because I got laid last night and they didn't. And I think about what Bill would say in a situation like this, and all of sudden I stand up and blurt out, as though Bill has taken me over, "How bout you two go and fuck yourselves! Okay?"

They both look stunned, then Brock jumps up and reaches for me. I leap back, and Trevor grabs Brocks big muscular arm, pulls him back toward the couch and says, "It's not worth it, Bro! You'll get kicked out of the house!" Brock rips his arm away from Trevor. My heart is pounding. I haven't been in a fight in a long time. I did break a kid's nose in the ninth grade, but he wasn't as big this jerkoff. Yet I'm ready to hold my own. I feel strangley *invincible* today.

"Wipe that smile off your fucking face, and be out of this house in an hour, or I swear to God, I'll hurt you," Brock spits out. And I believe him. I nod my head, and do a little curtsy bow to them, like Greg would sometimes do in the hospital. "As you desire, Lord Shithead," I say, turning toward the hallway.

"You're such a fucking weirdo," Trevor adds, shaking his head. I can't help but laugh.

I know Dr. Canter won't be proud of my aggressive behavior. But I know that Bill would, and that makes me smile.

I go back to my room. It looks like a room in a fraternity house that has been shut down and left abandoned. I'm glad to be getting out of this place. I just don't know where I'm going to go, as I don't have much money. Then I remember that I have a paycheck at work waiting for me to pick up. I can sleep in my car tonight, maybe get a room this weekend at the YMCA, or at least shower there. They allow the homeless to do that.

My roommate, Jaron, comes in as I'm packing. He's tall, thin and pale, with wire-rimmed glasses and a haircut similar to Spock's on *Star Trek*. He's quiet, and when you speak to him, it always looks like you've just interrupted him from reading a book.

"Are you leaving?" he asks me flatly, as though he's not surprised.

"Yes."

"Hey," Jaron says, a tinge of a smile crossing his lips. "Did you get lucky last night?"

I can't help but smile. "I wouldn't call it that, but yes, and something weird happened to me."

"Yeah. I bet a girl like that can shift your psyche," he says wistfully, like he's never been so lucky. He pauses for a second. "Did Brock try to extort money from you?"

"Yeah. What a prick." I answer as I stuff my clothes into my big green military bag.

"They do that to everyone. It's a racket," he says, shaking his head. "A guy who left before you came warned me about their scheme. They find a technicality to kick someone out on, then they try to extort them. They win either way though."

"How's that?" I'm packing as fast as I can to leave before the hour's up. I don't want to fight Brock. He's bigger and meaner than me.

"See, there's always a waiting list of people trying to get into these houses, so they know they can fill your spot," Jaron says.

"Uh. Huh," I say, looking up at him as I reach under my bed to grab some things.

"And if they kick someone out, then the landlord kicks them back $150 and keeps the rest. That's why he lets them drink and get high."

"What a bunch of dicks," I say, shaking my head, wondering what I'm going to do now. I'm not feeling so invincible anymore. I think about calling Jennifer or my parents. But I don't want someone to bail me out. Then I think about my grandparents.

"Yeah. They know guys like us don't have a lot of options. So, they use that to their advantage." Jaron looks at me as though I match the description of down-and-out characters in a novel. "Do you need any help getting your things out to your car?" I've only got two bags.

"No. I can get them," I say. "Don't want them to think you're helping me."

"Well, good luck. I'm almost kind of jealous, really. This place sucks," Jaron says, and I grapple with my bags and make my way out the door, down the hall, and out of the house and to my car. Brock is standing on the porch. He flips me the finger. A real saint.

32.

Once I get my things in the trunk, I start driving, drifting through traffic and barely steering the car. I'm heading toward the part of town near my grandparents' house, seeking out the comfort of something familiar. The sun is slowly making its descent toward the horizon, warming my face through the windshield, as I worry again about my future. Their house is near Lake Merritt in Oakland, a small lake with ducks and geese that old people and kids like to feed with breadcrumbs. It's where my grandmother used to bring me when I was a kid. By the lake there are some quaint little shops: a bar, a couple of restaurants, and a diner.

As I pass by the bar that looks like an old English pub, I have a sudden urge to stop off and get a drink. It's emotionally stressed-out days when I especially feel like drinking to numb the feelings of despair. But I figure if I start, I won't stop, and then all bets are off really, as it's like playing Russian Roulette with chaos. Everything can go to shit real quick.

I park along the street near a pay phone and decide to call my mom to find the nursing home where my grandparents are living. I want to visit them before it gets too late in the day. Like hospitals, they must have visiting hours.

Even though Lake Merritt is a pretty decent neighborhood, the pay phone is covered in graffiti, with a piece of chewed-up gum stuck to it. I wipe down the phone with my sweatshirt. The sun is starting to fade out, and the *fear* and anxiety are starting to kick back in. I hear a couple of geese honking, which calms me down, as calling home always makes me a little uncomfortable. I don't want to worry my mom, so I close my eyes and take a deep breath, like we did in our meditation practice at the hospital and say the mantra, *I am the captain of my ship and the master of my destiny.* I click the silver lever of the payphone, clearing the line. Then I wait for the dial tone and press 0.

"Operator. How can I help you?" a woman asks, her tone rather curtly.

"I'd like to make a collect call, please."

She gets mom's number and my name and calls. Mom accepts the call.

"Jackson. How are you? Is everything alright?"

"I'm good, Mom. I was just driving by Lake Merritt and started thinking of grandma and grandpa and wanted to visit them."

"I can hear the ducks in the background," mom says. I look over and see a little kid in red overalls running after a group of them.

"That's a lovely idea, Jackson. They've been asking about you. I know they're worried. But I told them that you're doing fine." She

pauses. "You know your father and I are proud of you."

"Thanks, Mom."

"Okay. The name of the nursing home is Sunset Manor. I

don't have the address in front of me, but you can look it up. It's

right across the street from that place grandma used to take you to

get ice cream. Do you remember where that is?"

"I remember." I would get a banana split with whip cream

and a cherry, every time I went there.

"I'll tell your father that you called."

"Okay. Thanks, Mom."

"Take care of yourself, Jackson."

Clouds on the horizon are threatening to cover up the sun,

and it's getting a little cooler out. I hang up the phone, pull my

hoodie up over my head for warmth, then pull up the phone book

with its plastic binder hanging by a slinky metal cord. A lot of the

pages are ripped out, including the one I need. I look around the

block and spot the diner on the corner. They'll have a phone book.

As I push open the glass door of the diner, the bell rings

above my head. I look around the diner. It's fairly empty. Some old-timers sit in booths next to the floor-to-ceiling windows that look out over Lake Merritt, drinking coffee, reading the newspaper, or talking to others. None of them look up at me. As I walk over to the curved, coffee-stained acrylic counter, lined with black vinyl swivel chairs—the wood backs nicked, the vinyl with fabric cuts—I have a strange feeling of deja vu, like I've been here before. Maybe I used to stop off here with my grandmother for Hot Chocolate. Either way, it feels comfortable. As I sit down in one of the chairs, I spin around trying to get my bearings.

A waitress about my age appears behind the counter. She's tall, with dirty-blonde hair, and a glint in her eyes. She's wearing a faded pink apron with a PJ Harvey button on the corner, her own personal 'flare.' Her hazel eyes peer at me and don't flinch.

"You need a menu, or are you just gonna take up space?" she asks with a smirk that belies her kind eyes.

"You get that a lot?" I ask.

She gives me a more thorough examination, like she's dissecting me. It's unnerving. I now realize that I haven't washed today or combed my hair or anything, and that I probably look like a derelict. I run my hand through my hair trying to pat it down.

"Sometimes," she finally adds.

I smile. "Could I just get a cup of coffee and the phone book please?"

"Please. Now that's original." She smiles, turns, and walks down to the other end of the counter to the coffee urns.

She brings back the coffee cup as well as a couple of creamers and sets them down in front of me.

I lean back in the black vinyl chair and smile to myself. I'm in the middle of something that feels like *living*, and it feels good.

"What are *you* so smiley about?" she asks, probing.

"Nothing, really. It's just that . . . this moment feels comfortable."

She shakes her head. *Are you for real?* She then peers at me more closely, trying to figure me out, I assume.

"Sorry about that." I pause, reigning it back in. "Could I just get that phone book too?"

"You're not from around here, are you?" she asks, probing again.

I wonder if she can see that I'm just recently homeless and just got out of a mental hospital? Or, does she somehow see what

I've been asking myself: Who am I, *really*? I remember an article in National Geographic, by a scientist who said, "Things may not exist until someone *sees* it." Or something like that. Anyway, that's kind of how I feel right now.

"Uhm, no . . ." I stammer, "but my grandparent's house is just around the corner. Used to come here in the summertime to visit."

"Oh." She purses her lips. Raises one of her eyebrows. "Then why don't you go there and use their phone book?"

"Well, they don't live there anymore . . ." I smile at her. She's playing with me. I don't think she thinks I'm crazy anymore.

She crosses her arms and smiles. "Are you trying to find them then?"

"Yeah, sort of, actually."

"Really," she says and looks at me as though I'm lying. "Where did they go?"

I sigh. She's like a damn detective. "Do you *usually* question everybody who asks for your phone book?"

"No," she says, "Just suspicious-looking customers." I smile as I know I must look it. She doesn't let me hang. "The payphone book out there is all torn up. *So,* we always get a lot of weirdos in here asking for ours. Caught one guy tearing out pages once."

I laugh. "I bet he'll never do that again." I wouldn't cross her.

"Got that right, buddy." She pauses. Still curious it seems. "So, where are your grandparents, anyway?"

"They're actually in a nursing home, and I'm just trying to find a phone number, so I can go visit them," I blurt out, feeling a little exhausted now.

"Ohhh . . ." she says totally surprised. "Why didn't you say so? That's sweet." She now reaches out and touches my hand. "I feel bad for grilling you like that."

"It's okay. I kind of like it."

She smirks. "Let's not get ahead of ourselves." She steps over to the cash register, bends over, her skirt hiking up her legs. I look away. She grabs the book, stands up, and looks back at me. Must've seen my head turned away. I turn back. She smiles. "Aren't we the proper gentleman."

She now marches down to the end of the counter and waves me over. "Come over here and look up the name!" I walk down to the end of the counter. She sets the phone book down and hands me their portable phone. I sit down and look up at her. I now realize that she's not classically pretty, like Jennifer, but has her own unique, natural beauty.

"What do you do, besides working here?" I ask.

She smiles at me. "Theater. I'm studying to be an actress. What about you?"

"I'm going to be a writer."

"I should've figured as much. We're trained to observe suspicious behavior," she says.

I laugh. "What's your name?"

"Lacy. And yours?"

"Jackson."

"Nice to meet you Jackson, the writer. Hope you're not one of those stream-of-consciousness artists." I look puzzled. "I mean, you know, like the painter Jackson Pollock."

I laugh, feeling like this is one of those chance encounters that could change everything. "No. I'm much more together than someone like him."

She looks at my hair, then searches my eyes. "Uh, huh," she says, unconvincingly.

I open the phone book and find the number for Sunset Manors.

"Are you ready?" She looks up at me.

I nod, pick up the gray cordless phone that she's set in front of me, and punch out the number.

"Sunset Manors. How can I help you?" an older woman asks.

"Yes, hi. I'm calling about your visiting hours. I'd like to come and see my grandparents, Mr. and Mrs. George Smith."

"Oh, yes. They're lovely. Visiting times are five to seven on weekdays and noon to five on Saturday's and Sunday's."

We exchange goodbyes and I hang up the phone. I look up at Lacy. She's smiling. Waiting. "Visiting hours are from five to seven." She turns and looks at the clock hanging above the service counter. "It's almost six o'clock now. You better get going."

"Yeah, you're right. I need to go."

"Come back and see me, Jackson," she says, smiling. "I want to know how the visit went. And," she starts to say, almost blushing.

"And, by the way, I'm in a small play opening Friday night, if you wanted to come?"

"Sure. Yeah, of course." I stand up to leave, then turn back. "Where's the play at?"

"Oh, yeah. Hold on . . ." She says, then reaches down and pulls a flyer out from underneath the counter. She smiles and hands it to me, "it's just a small part, really..." I stop her, "I'll be there!" And I run out the door.

33.

When I leave the diner it's colder outside than I expected, and I rush to my car. The sky is turning dark and it's getting late. And as much as I want to go and see my grandparents, I realize that I'll have to go another time, because I really need a place to stay tonight. It's too cold to sleep in my car.

I decide I better try to get a room at the YMCA, at least for the night. I remember Steven telling me that you only have to fill out an application for long-term stays.

I need the address to the Y, but I can't go back inside and ask Lacy to use the phone book again; I don't want to spook her.

Besides, I'm starting to feel a little rundown as it's been a long day. I look around at the shops. The wind kicks up, and people huddle themselves as they pass me on the sidewalk. Leaves blow down the streets. I see a small bookstore at the other end of the block. I grab my coat out of the back, put it on, then hurry down the sidewalk to get quickly out of the wind.

The door to the bookstore closes with a *whoosh*. The old woman behind the counter, with silver hair, a blue sweater, and reading glasses hanging around her neck, gives me a warm smile.

"It's nice to see that young people still read. Looking for anything in particular?"

"Just the meaning of life and a place to sleep," I tell her.

She laughs. "Oh my, well, I can't help you with a place to sleep, but a bookstore is about as good a place as any to get answers about the meaning of life."

"I'll see what I can find."

"Good luck, son."

I look around the store until I come to the travel section. I find a guidebook to Oakland, but the YMCA isn't listed. I walk back to the counter.

"Did you find the answer already?" the old woman asks with a sly smile.

"No, but I've got prospects." I pause. "However, I do need to find a place to sleep tonight. Do you have a phone book?"

"Yes, but the YMCA is just up the road on Broadway. I hear it's clean, and the people there are friendly." Old people always seem to know about the YMCA. My grandpa used to exercise there.

"Thanks, you're a godsend."

She gives me directions, and then reaches down and pulls up a used copy of the *Oakland Chronicle* and hands it to me. "Here's something to read," she adds with a twinkle in her eyes. "I have a good feeling about you, that you just might solve that question of yours."

"Let's pray!" I say, as I push out the door into the wind, thinking that Steven would be proud of me.

It's nearly dark outside by the time I get to the YMCA. I park the car in their lot and grab the newspaper off the passenger's seat, my backpack from the backseat with my overnight things, and head toward the glass doors of the Y, bracing myself against the cold.

Inside it's warm. The lobby is white, minimal, and clean. It's also airy and spacious. And I can see why Steven with all his internal chaos would like this place. YMCA posters with upcoming classes and events are posted on a community board along the wall to my right. There's a plant on the check-in desk, and behind it a middle-aged man wearing a blue polo shirt, with a red Y on it.

"The space is nice, isn't it?" he says, as though reading my mind. "It was recently done over."

"It's better than I was expecting . . ."

"I understand," he says, smiling. "Were you expecting the *Village People* singing Y.M.C.A! in their feather boas, black leather, and policeman outfits, and perhaps a disco in full swing?"

I laugh. "Something like that."

"We get that all the time. Don't worry. So, you'd like a room then?"

"Yes. I really need a room, if you have one available. And not just for tonight, but maybe long-term."

"Well, you've come to the right place. A single room for the night is $30, and a single room monthly is $250. For the room tonight, I'll just need to see your ID."

"Okay." I hand him my ID and the money.

"And for the monthly room, I'll give you the application to fill out. You'll just need a current pay stub and a personal reference."

"Great."

"Just return this with your paystub, and we'll hold the room for you. Showers are at the end of your hallway." He hands me a key and my ID. "You'll be in room number seven tonight, and the desk clerk tomorrow can tell you about all the amenities, like the gym, pool, and classes." I nod my head. He smiles. "And the disco starts at midnight."

"Great. Gives me enough time to unpack my dancing shoes."

He laughs, as I walk down the hall.

Once I'm in the room and settled, I realize that I'm starving, but I'm too tired to go back out. Maybe they have a snack machine downstairs, I think, but doubt if they serve late-night snacks like at the hospital. I sit on the bed and open the *Oakland Chronicle*. On the third page is a large, green advertisement that reads, "Oakland Writer's Workshop/Sign up today while spots are still available/Six-month workshop/Submission of a thirty-page manuscript is required/Admission based on submission." The deadline for the submission is Friday.

The old lady must have been an angel sent from Heaven? I think about calling Steven, and telling him that I think he's onto something with the God thing, but it's probably too late. I'll call him later this week.

I don't have much time, but I know I've got to follow up on this *divine intervention,* as Steven would say. I remember the term *synchronicity* from one of my psych courses in school and feel like my life is *finally* clicking. I set the newspaper aside, lean over and grab my backpack. I unzip it and pull out my yellow notepads and pens from the hospital with all of my journal pages. I sit back up on the bed and write at the top of the notepad, *Hospital Eyes.* Tomorrow after work, I'll go to the Oakland Library and use one of their computers to start rewriting my journal entries from the hospital. I'm sure I can pull together thirty pages. Jennifer would be proud of me, I think.

The next day, when I get off work, the sun is shining outside the windows of the coffee shop. A song is playing with the chorus, *Sail away, Sail away, Sail away*, and I feel like I could. Even though I made so many cappuccinos and lattes that my brain is numb and my clothes are stained with milk, I feel alive now that I have a new direction, and a new place to live. Today is the first day of my new life, like they often said in hospital, and I need to focus. First, I need to fill out my application to the YMCA, then I need to go to the library and start writing my submission.

It's quiet in the coffee shop, besides the background music, and fairly empty. I settle in at a table in the corner. The application doesn't take long. I now ask the assistant manager if I can use the phone in the office. He nods his head, and I go back and call Dr. Canter, leaving a message that I used her as a reference for a room at the YMCA. I don't think she'll mind. As I gather up my things from the table Jennifer walks in. She gives me a weak smile and my heart sinks a little. I know what's coming and I sit back down, already feeling a tinge of heartbreak.

After Jennifer and I talked, each recognizing that we had a fun night, but that we come from two different worlds, and each need to follow our seperate lives and wished each other the best and hugged and all that crap, I leave the coffee shop feeling a little raw, just trying to stay focused on getting the writing that I need to get done.

As I walk to my car in the warmth of the sun, a sudden feeling of gratitude comes over me, pushing out the dark thoughts that are never too far off. That word, gratitude, was used a lot in the hospital, and it drove me crazy at first, but I realize that I really am grateful to be out of the hospital and out of the halfway house, and maybe even out of the YMCA soon. I'm grateful that I feel like I have a *life* again.

At the YMCA I turn in my application, along with my paystub to the friendly, slightly effeminate guy with wispy blonde hair and baby-blue glasses behind the desk. A weathered old man in a wool hat and brown sweater sits next to a fern silently staring out the lobby windows.

"Okay. Great," the Y clerk says, looking over my paperwork, then glancing up at me. "It looks like you have everything we need. How long are you wanting to rent a room for?"

"For six months. Is that possible?"

"Sure," he says cheerily. "Six, nine, twelve. Whatever works best for you, as long as your reference checks out." He looks down at my paperwork. "A Dr. Canter…? We'll give them a call tomorrow."

"Sounds good."

The old man by the window looks over at us. "Oh, just let the young man have the room Phillip," he says to the attendant. "I'll be his reference. He looks like a perfectly fine young fellow. Can't be any crazier than the characters we've already got roaming around this place." He laughs loudly at this remark.

"Yes. Thank you for the help, William," Phillip says, rolling his eyes.

William laughs and goes back to staring out the window.

"So, you'll just have to pay for tonight, then I can show you around the facilities," Phillip adds and waves his hand in a circle above his head as though he were in a beauty pageant. "You'll have full access next door to our gym, pool, and basketball court."

But before he continues, I stop him. I'm getting anxious. I *need* to get writing. "Is it possible to take a look at all of that later in the week? I've got a deadline on a writing submission and I need to get started on it."

Phillip trains his eyes back on me. "Oh, sure. Yes, I understand. You can take a look at all the facilities whenever you want. No pressure at all. So, you're you a writer, huh?"

"Not yet. I want to *be* a writer."

"Well, William over here is a writer as well," Phillip says. "Isn't that right, William?" The old man gives us a grave look, grunts and then nods his head.

"I'm trying to get into a writer's workshop," I add.

"Well, you look interesting to me. So, I'm expecting the next great American novel from you soon! If you need to buy groceries or coffee or anything, there's a convenience store just down the block. And we do have a kitchen and lounge area back there." Phillip points over his shoulder. "If you need anything, you just let me know. Okay?"

"Okay. Thanks." I hurry toward the doors. As I cross the lobby to the glass doors, William looks up at me with his heavy eyes and says matter-of-factly, "So, you're a writer, eh?"

I stop and turn to him, "No, not yet. Not really. But I'm trying."

"Do you know what Jack Kerouac said about writing?" he asks me, studying my face. But before I can answer, he continues, "You look like you may have suffered a little bit. It's in your eyes. That's a good thing if you want to be a writer." He looks down for a moment as though lost in thought, then glances back up at me. "Kerouac said that every book he wrote was a love letter to the world . . . Think about that. That's beautiful and sad at the same time. Isn't it?"

I think about it for a second, "Yes, it is."

At the library, I get a library card and sort myself out. I have at least four hours today to work on the submission before the library closes at 7:00. So, I seat myself at an available computer along a row of them in the middle of the first floor. A pale white light shines in from the large windows that surround the massive bookcases. I take out all of my yellow journaling notepads from the hospital and set them on the desk next to the computer. As I do, the flyer for Lacy's play this Friday falls out onto the floor. I pick it up and smile, as it pushes my talk with Jennifer further out of my mind. I'm looking forward to seeing her play and hoping that I can convince her to have a drink with me afterward, put *her* on the witness stand this time.

I start rereading my journal entries, thinking of how I want to make sense of it all. I reflexively take a deep breath and think back to how this all started, how I ended up *here,* and *where* I want to start my narrative. An image arises of me lying in the bed of my room in the Intensive Care Unit of the hospital with the overhead fluorescent lights flickering on and off, thinking about Aaron and the demons, whispering, watching me. I start to write, and it begins to flow out of me. Hours later I look over and see a girl sitting across from me, staring at me as though she can't figure out if I'm a mad typist or just a little off, as I start laughing, remembering how Aaron convinced that typing was the only useful skill we were learning in high school. I smile at her and continue typing.

I type and type until the sun starts fading from the library windows and until the nice old woman in her Sunday church service clothes comes around and tells me that it's time to go. I gather the fifteen pages I've written and realize that it's going to take at least another afternoon here to complete my 30-page submission. Plus, I'll have to do some editing at night in my room at the Y.

On Friday, I take the submission to a Kinko's and have it bound and put into a large manila envelope and take it directly to the office of the Oakland Writer's Association located in a large, imposing building in downtown Oakland. The office is on the fourth floor, and I'm so worried since it's late afternoon that I might miss the deadline that I bound up the stairs like a gazelle.

When I make it to the fourth floor, I'm gasping for air. I lean against the wall in the corner, and I take in the layout of the floor. It's an open plan of wrought iron, and wood and glass, so that you can see the entirety of the cubicles on the floor with windows that look out over the bay to San Francisco. It sends chills down my spine, and for the second time in a week, I have an overwhelming sense of deja-vu.

Muffled conversation and the ringing of telephones fills the air, and I feel a sinking sensation in my stomach, as though I may be out of my league here. I sit down on one of the wood benches near the stairwell to catch my breath and calm my anxiety. I worry that I may just be a crazy, delusional mental patient who was told that he had talent as a writer simply to help build up my self-esteem. Am I holding my future in the manila envelope or a laughable rambling pipedream of a madman? Then I think about Aaron, and what a great writer he could have been, and I *swear* I hear his voice say, "I believe in you, buddy." I stand up and walk over to the reception desk.

35.

After I hand over the manuscript with my contact information, I'm told that they'll get back to me in a couple of days. Lacy's playhouse is only six blocks away and the performance starts at 7:00. I'm starving and need to find a place to eat. As I push out the doors into the cool gray day I think about Lacy's cheeky smile, her sarcasm... I felt like she saw right through me that day… I feel like she believed me when I said that I was a writer, and the air hangs crystaline, full of the optism of possiblity that I haven't felt in a long time. And I'm glad to be alive.

After dinner I feel electric walking down the sidewalk toward the theater, with the twilight turning to night. The playhouse is a small converted store, next to a couple of bars and restaurants with a few people standing outside talking and smoking. The play is starting soon, and I maneuver through the bodies and make it to the ticket table, protecting the rose that I'm carrying against my chest.

"One ticket please."

"Oh, you brought a rose! Aren't you such a gentleman!" the woman says to me, smiling broadly, and I picture Aaron laughing.

Inside, lights hang from the low ceiling, illuminating its black tar paper. There are forty or so folding chairs set out, and I sit in the back row. The stage is only a few feet higher, but tall enough for everybody to see the actors.

The house lights begin to flicker, and the others take their seats. There is a hush in the crowd as the play begins.

Then, Lacy comes out onstage, the spotlight finding her, glowing with charisma, and she stops in the middle of the stage in an antique 18th century dress. She starts to talk about her life in Norway in a loveless marriage and her experience of missing out on life. The woman next to me says, "Ah, Ibsen, don't you love him." I nod, unfamiliar with the playwright, but mesmerized by the lead actress and her performance.

After a standing ovation, I wait in my seat until most of the audience has cleared out. A few of the actors have come back out on stage and are talking to people from the audience. And when it becomes obvious that Lacy isn't coming back out, I walk up to the stage and ask one of the other actresses if she'll give the rose to her.

"That's so sweet," she says, taking the rose.

"Tell her it's from Jackson, and that I'll be out front if she's free to get a drink."

"Okay, Jackson. I'll tell her," she says with an alluring smile, as if to say, 'if she won't, I will.' The girl crosses the stage, looking back at me as she pushes through the curtain as though she's trying to figure out who I am. And I wonder if Lacy has a boyfriend.

I stand outside for what seems like an eternity, until I finally hear my name, like church bells ringing, "Hey, Jackson!" I turn to see Lacy walking towards me, her dirty blond hair falling down over the collar of her long, blue wool coat. She's wearing a long white dress underneath and flat black shoes. Her lips are stained red and her mascara light blue. She's holding my rose, and she looks stunning.

"Aren't you going to say something?" Lacy asks as she approaches, breaking my trance.

"*Yes.* You look stunning! And . . . your performance was amazing!" I say, trying to regain my composure.

"Better than at the diner?" she asks with a sly smile.

"Better material."

She smiles. "Yes, the classics. Not very hip, but deep and honest." I nod my head. My lack of a fine art education betraying me.

Lacy senses my awkwardness and holds up the rose. "This was very sweet of you. So, thank you. But it was also very bold. How do you know I don't have a boyfriend?" she asks, twirling the rose in her left hand.

"It was in appreciation of your performance, boyfriend or not."

She now steps very close, and I feel her warm sweet breath on my face.

She laughs, "I was hoping you would come."

"I'm glad I did. As you said, the play had depth. I liked it. I could identify with the woman's sorrow."

Lacy looks at me with those penetrating eyes, seeing more than I wish, but not flinching. "*You* have depth, Jackson."

She takes my arm and tosses her head back. "So! Where are we going?"

"Well, would you like to get a drink?"

"I'd love to get a drink, but I don't have a fake ID. Maybe dessert?" We start walking arm and arm, and she sidles up next to me. "Who knows. If I like what I hear, I might even let you kiss me goodnight."

"What more could a guy ask for?" I smile.

Lacy giggles a bit, and squeezes my arm, "Oh, Jackson...you're quite the charmer," she says, in her thick Norweigan accent from the play.

I look over at her and realize that whatever becomes of my desire to be a writer, or even my desire for Lacy - I have arrived and I'm ready for my new life.

"You got that right, Buddy," I smile a little to myself and realize that it's me doing the talking now.

84200256R00156